CW00457333

Ironshield's Shadow: Book 3
The Book of Life
JB Caine
with
Lea Scism and Sam Hamilton

Table of Contents

The Arcana Series (YA Paranormal)
Rise of the Moon
Rush to Judgement
Strength of Will (coming in 2024)

Ironshield's Shadow (High Fantasy)
Book 1: Beginnings
Book 2: The Book of Order
Book 3: The Book of Life

Short Stories (Horror)
"The Hit" in *Autumn Tales (Anatolian Press)*
"Kinvarra" in *Autumn Tales II (Anatolian Press)*

Short Stories (Dark Fantasy/Myth Retellings)
"Hidden Soul Beneath" in *Wicked Ever After*
(Grim House Publishing)
"Line of Succession: in Forgotten Lore
(Grim House Publishing)

Follow JB Caine on social media!
Website: www.jbcaine.com
Instagram: @authorjbcaine
Facebook: @realjbcaine

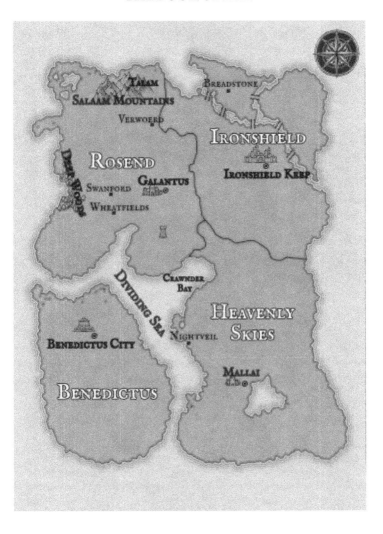

Chapter 1

A Dark Confrontation

Dalgis

Learning to read was hard work.

Fortunately, Argus had some experience in teaching his children, and so his patience seemed to be infinite. He had spent two days' travel teaching Dalgis how to recognize the 28 letters in the Dyosan alphabet and, while some of them looked so much alike that he confused them fairly often, Dalgis beamed with pride anytime Argus praised his efforts.

"A very fine effort indeed, Dalgis."

"I promise you I am paying attention, Argus. I just keep confusing the one with the squiggle on the top for the one with the squiggle on the bottom."

"Don't be so hard on yourself, my friend. I've never known a human child to learn the alphabet in two days," Argus smiled as he patted the beast's colorful feathers. "We'll give it another day of practice, and then we'll start with some basic words that you'll see a great deal on signs and such. You are a very fine student."

Dalgis ruffled his plumage and grinned a very pointy and joyful grin. "Where is it that we're going again?"

"Ah, that is the question, isn't it? We're heading north, and that's really all we know at the moment. Fufei seemed to think that the clues were pointing toward the region where the storm elves dwell."

"I've never seen a storm elf, I don't believe. What do they look like?"

"I have seen one, though it's been many years. In physique, they look like sun elves: relatively slender with angular features. But storm elves are very fair-skinned, and their hair is white, gray, or black; their eyes are usually some shade of blue or gray.

"Breadstone, where I'm from, is in the northern part of Ironshield, and the Salaam Mountains, where the storm elves live, is in the northern part of Rosend. Before Godfroy cut off trade routes with Rosend, we used to trade with the storm elves: grain for lumber. I was only a boy then, but I remember it because it was, to my young mind, an odd arrangement. A few farmers from our town would collect wagons full of grain and haul it out to the Ironshield/Rosend border at the end of the harvest season. I was allowed to go along one time in my youth so that I could understand the arrangement. The storm elves would show up at the meeting place with the same number of wagons full of lumber. We'd swap cargo with them, have a silent meal together as a symbol of honorable commerce, then return to our places of origin."

"A silent meal? Were there no stories told around a fire? No music? A silent meal seems an odd way to show fellowship." Dalgis shook his head in confusion.

"It is odd, I suppose, but the storm elves don't generally speak any language but their own; very few of them bother to even learn Dyosa. The silent meal is meant to show that even in our differences, we can find common ground and serve each other. It's rather poetic, I think."

Dalgis nodded slowly. "I still prefer stories and music."

Argus chuckled. "It's about time for us to break camp and begin our travels, but I'd like to have a look at Xezia's map and see where we are in relation to where we're going. Would you care to come along and practice your letter identification?"

"Oh, most definitely! I shall not let the squiggles defeat me!"

They found Xezia hunched over his map and Sora shaking with laughter.

"Damnable bird!" Xezia swore.

"BIIRRRRDD!" Squealer screeched from a tree behind Xezia.

"What's going on here, comrades?" asked Dalgis.

"This creature keeps diving at me," Xezia growled, looking over his shoulder at the black bird.

Sora struggled to contain her mirth at his apparent misfortune. "It seems Squealer here has taken a liking to the map. Ever since Xezia pulled it out of his bag this morning, our feathered friend has been trying to make off with it."

"Might be nice if *someone* stood guard," he grumbled.

"What? And miss the show? Surely you jest."

"I shall stand watch for you, Xezia," Dalgis offered, "so that you and Argus can plot our course for the day."

"Finally, a little assistance!" Xezia shot a sidelong glance at Sora, but seeing her grin, he seemed to soften and the anger melted away.

Dalgis extended his neck until he was eye-to-eye with the bird, who seemed more amused than put off by the confrontation. "We'll take no more shenanigans from you, bird. We are on an important mission!" Squealer cawed back with a sound that resembled laughter, and hopped from the branch onto Dalgis's beaky snout. "At least I can keep an eye on you if you're going to perch there."

Satisfied that Squealer's mischief was under control, Xexia unrolled the map across his lap. "So, Argus, do you still feel as though this is the correct route? Your target takes us awfully close to the Ironshield border."

Argus nodded. "Your concern is well-founded, and there may be any number of issues as we enter this area at the base of the mountains. I imagine we might encounter well-armed residents, and might even run across scouting parties of Ironshield soldiers. I'm hoping to get some information here in Verwoerd." He pointed to a dot on the map. "It's the only town I know in this region of Rosend, and one of the few places humans won't be detained on sight. I stopped through there on my way to Wheatfields, and there are a few folks in town there who know me. I've also asked my wife to send a package of supplies to the tavern owner there, as I've run through some of what I'd packed. I had no idea I'd be away for so long." There was a hint of sadness in his voice that hurt Dalgis's huge heart. "From Verwoerd, we should head into the Salaam Mountains here..."

As Argus pointed toward the target area on the map, Squealer dropped off of Dalgis's nose and dove toward the men. He zipped under Argus's arm and snatched the map out of Xezia's grip.

"Damn!" Xezia swore again. "Give me that map, you stupid bird, or I'll have Argus make a very small stew out of you!"

Squealer set the map in the crotch of branches and let out a cackle. He flapped his wings and preen himself as he kept one eye on the people far below him.

"Looks like your nemesis won," Sora chuckled.

Xezia shot her a look, but said nothing.

"What in the world is going on over here?" Ekko asked, as she and the rest of the party approached, having packed up all their gear. "Are we headed out or what?"

Xezia pointed silently at the smug mynah bird.

"Huh. You want me to kill him?" Ekko reached for the blowgun she had strapped to her thigh.

"That would be lovely, thank you. But the map would still be way up there."

"Oh, there is that," she shrugged.

"My deepest apologies, Xezia. Squealer was much quicker than I expected." Dalgis hung his head.

"Do we really need the map?" Ren asked. "We've certainly looked at it enough to know where we're going for now. Perhaps we could obtain another."

"I'd really prefer to have that one back," Xezia said. "It was given to me by...a friend."

"*FRIEEEENND!*" Squealer cawed, and all eyes turned toward him. He hopped from one foot to the other, then nudged the edge of the map until it rolled itself back up.

"Now what do you suppose he's up to?" Dalgis wondered aloud.

As if in response, the bird cocked its head to the side and grabbed the map with its beak.

"Don't you dare!" cried Xezia, but it was too late. Squealer launched out of the tree with the map and lit on another branch about 50 feet away. He set the map down carefully and screeched again. "*FRIEEEEND!*"

Xezia seethed in exasperation, but Dalgis saw something else in the bird's behavior. "Hold on a moment, friends. I do believe he wants us to follow him!" Squealer cocked his head to one side. "It appears he's waiting for us."

"You've got to be joking. The last thing I want is to follow that demon bird into the woods, away from any discernible path," Xezia complained.

"It doesn't appear we have much choice if you want your map," Ekko pointed out as she climbed nimbly on to Dalgis's back.

Xezia growled in exasperation, but started trudging toward where Squealer had landed. The rest of the party followed. As they drew near, the bird picked up the map and flew another 70 feet deeper into the forest, then landed again and waited.

And so it continued for nearly half an hour, with Xezia's curses growing more vehement and creative as time passed.

"It appears there's something up ahead," Dalgis reported from his higher vantage point. "I believe we're about to find out where he's leading us."

"It's about bloody time."

Dalgis could see that the bird had landed on something lower than a tree...perhaps a signpost...and stayed perched there with the map in his beak.

"What in the world?" exclaimed Daijera.

As they approached the post, Squealer looked down at them expectantly. The sign had clearly once been a marker identifying the name of the place that now became visible before them, but the words were obscured by dark burn marks, as though the word had been deliberately scorched off. Squealer dropped the map, flew up to a tree limb, and yipped in satisfaction.

Despite a lack of any sort of path, it was clear that they had found a small settlement, though it seemed it had been untenanted for some time. The forest should have begun to reclaim the buildings, but no ivy crept up the sides, and no weeds were growing through cracks in what appeared to be cobbled streets. Were it not for the surrounding forest, it would look like a typical town square, albeit an empty one.

"Does this seem odd to anyone else?" Sora asked. "I mean, look here. It goes from dirt here," she pointed at their feet, "to the road right there by the sign. Doesn't that seem abrupt? Shouldn't there be a road leading up to the sign? Even a few bricks?"

Argus narrowed his eyes, nodding. "There is something very wrong about this place."

"You have a gift for stating the obvious," Daijera quipped, but then seemed to think better of picking a fight. "It appears to be abandoned, though. Do you think there's something here we're supposed to find?"

"Only one way to find out, friends!" Dalgis chuffed, excited for a new adventure. "Let us investigate!"

From the tree above, the mynah bird's croaky chuckle echoed down as the group set foot on the cobbled road, one by one.

Ekko

Ekko held tight to Dalgis as they stepped into the abandoned square. It appeared to be a common area like those in many towns, with a statue and fountain in the center, ringed by business establishments of one sort or another. The buildings were like many she'd seen, constructed of whitewashed stone with heavy wooden doors. The few windows were small with shutters on either side to keep out the chill in the wintertime. A wagon wheel leaned against the wall of the closest building and the wide doors were slightly ajar. Even beyond the apparent emptiness, something niggled at her from the back of Ekko's mind, but the idea wouldn't take shape.

"What's the matter with this place?" she asked aloud, hoping someone else could fill in the blanks she couldn't.

"There appear to be no houses, for one," Ren commented. A hazy mist seemed to cling to everything, despite the sun's rays. "How can you have a town square with no citizens living nearby?"

Dalgis scanned the trees, an uncharacteristic unease furrowing his brow. "I don't care for it here," he said, tension thrumming through his voice. "And the other animals don't either. Listen...all the bird sounds are coming from the trees. None from the village. You'd expect there would be nests in the eaves."

"BIIIRRRD!" Squealer screeched from the treeline.

Ekko's alert ears perked up as a cool breeze filled with whispers blew through the street. She shivered, though she wasn't sure if it was from the wind or the disembodied voices it carried.

"Did you hear that?" asked Daijera. "Please tell me you heard that."

"We heard it," said Ren, drawing his sword. "I think we need to be prepared for anything."

"I doubt that sword will do you much good against ghosts, Ren," Daijera commented.

"That's for Argus and Xezia to worry about. I fight what I can."

They crept forward carefully, keeping a watchful eye for movement. Sora peeked through the open door of the building as they passed.

"Looks like a one-stop shop for all things horse," she reported. "Big open bay, a couple of wagons on the right, and a smithy to the left. Doesn't look like it's been used in awhile, but it doesn't feel like death exactly, either."

Xezia's spun to face her. "What does that mean?"

Sora's eyes grew wide for a second, as though she'd revealed something she hadn't meant to. "I don't know...I guess I've been around places where people have died. This doesn't feel like that."

"Like where, exactly? Battlefields? Graveyards?"

"Both, actually. Maybe I'm crazy; I don't know." She looked back at the open doors and shrugged.

Xezia had stopped moving and was staring at her intently. She turned back and met his gaze.

"Oh, for all the skies, Xezia. It's not like that. I think it's because I spent a lot of time at a Hoshkn temple when I was younger. Death has a certain vibration to it. Even violent death. This place feels...different."

"Different how?"

She sighed, looking for the right word. "Unnatural. It feels unnatural."

"Yes!" Dalgis cried. "Just so! Unnatural!"

"Well, let's be on guard, then," Argus said quietly, making intricate gestures with his fingers. "I'm not picking up any traces of magic–even old magic–right here, but there's bound to be some somewhere."

"Right." Sora stepped forward first, giving Xezia a playful punch in the gut. "Let's see why this dumb bird brought us here. By the way, does anyone think *that* might be a little out of the ordinary? Annoying bird follows us from the Deep Woods, then leads us to a ghost town? Anyone?"

"I think it's fair to say our lives have taken on a strange turn ever since we all met," Ren replied.

The party continued forward toward the center of the square, where a dried-up fountain pool, about six feet in diameter lay below a statue of a shepherd and two sheep.

"The fountain has an aura of magic," Argus reported, "though I can't pinpoint its type or function."

As if in reply, the dry fountain began to gurgle from underneath. Dalgis craned his neck forward, allowing him to see its contents from a safe distance. "It's filling with a dark liquid." Ekko slid down from his back to take a closer look, and the rest of the group followed suit.

"What is that, oil?" she asked.

"Not oil," said Xezia, who looked even paler than usual. He took a step closer to Sora and put his hand out, as if to push her back if there was danger. "Stay back."

The viscous substance now filled the bottom of the pool, and the level was rising. As it reached the upper lip of the basin, it erupted into a cylindrical column reaching toward the sky. Up, up, up it went, mocking gravity. The whispers returned, only now they sounded like distant shrieking, their origins deep within the column of blackness. Ekko covered her ears.

"Why does it look like that?" she yelled above the cacophony. It didn't resemble any liquid she'd ever seen; it seemed to absorb light rather than reflecting it.

The surface of the inky substance rippled and it seemed to her that she could almost make out faces in the darkness. Agonized faces that were almost familiar...

You are a complete failure as a thief, Ekko. How do you expect to help support this family with the pittance you bring in? Your sister is three years younger than you, and she brings home twice as much stuff.

That should be more than enough, then. You don't need me risking my neck to pick pockets in town.

Stop being contrary, you ungrateful snipe! Wait a minute...what's that in your pocket?

Nothing. A rock I picked up for luck.

A rock for luck? Of all the idiocy. Give it here. Hold still! Well, well, a rock, you say? This rock looks a bit like a bejeweled locket! What else have you been holding onto? Keeping the best loot for yourself, are you?

So what if I kept something? I'm entitled to a better cut. You send me out to the riskiest places.

Entitled? You're barely entitled to the breath I gave you, you little brat! How dare you...

"Noooo!" Ekko screamed, falling to the ground and pulling her eyes away from the undulating faces. She stayed very still, willing her breath and heartbeat to slow, before looking up at the other members of the party.

Ren had fallen to his knees, one arm outstretched and the other over his heart. "I'm sorry...so sorry...I failed you..." he muttered, tears welling in his eyes.

Daijera stared impudently into the black mass, as if daring it to attack, but her left hand was gripped in a white-knuckled fist.

Xezia had thrown his cloak around Sora, shielding her from seeing whatever horrors the fountain held for her. He yelled unintelligibly at the column of liquid, his fingers crackling with electricity and reaching for the darkness.

Argus stood stock still, eyes closed, slowly breathing in and out.

Elia swung her arms, as if fighting invisible foes, screaming, "No! It's not my fault! Not my fault!"

And Dalgis, sweet Dalgis, stamped his feet and bellowed, clearly in agony such that he could not form words.

And then, as quickly as it appeared, the column rumbled and sucked itself back toward the basin, the voices howling as Xezia howled back.

And then all was quiet again, and the blackness was gone.

Broken from their visions, everyone remained silent for a moment. Then Argus asked, "Is everyone quite alright?"

"My father...I saw him in that darkness...asking me why I hadn't protected him. Why, with all my strength, I had not saved him..." Dalgis lay down, his head on the cobblestones, tears streaming down his cheeks. Ekko went and put her arms around his neck, patting him soothingly. He sniffled and leaned into her, welcoming the comfort.

No one else seemed inclined to share what they had seen, and Ekko was glad. It wasn't as though she had forgotten that night, or the beating she'd gotten following her mother's discovery. But she had left her home that night and never returned, and she didn't even wish to look back on it in memory.

Putting her own experience together with what Dalgis had said, she ventured a theory. "I think maybe that...whatever...shoved us back into our worst memory."

"Something like that," Daijera said slowly. "But it was a warped version of the memory. Like it wanted me to feel bad about it. But I don't." Everyone turned to her, awaiting an explanation. She didn't offer one.

Sora disentangled herself from Xezia's cloak. "Xezia, what in the world was all that gibberish? I mean, I appreciate the protection and all, but..."

"What do you mean gibberish? I was telling it to stay back, to leave us alone. And I was praying to Epi for help."

"In what language?"

Xezia looked confused. "I thought I was speaking Dyosa, but I guess I might have been speaking something else..."

"You sounded like you were making the same sounds *it* was," Ekko commented, "though I guess I'm not an expert in that area."

"No, I, wait...you guys couldn't understand what it was saying?" A ripple of fear passed through his eyes, just briefly, and for an instant, Ekko saw a lost child as much as she saw the surly mage she'd gotten to know.

Sora seemed to notice it, too, her eyes softening. Then she leapt to her feet. "Oh, great day in the morning! Does this mean I owe you a DOUBLE blood debt?"

Relief and gratitude washed over his features, quickly replaced by the snarky grin that was so familiar to them all. "Well, now that you mention it..."

Sora roared in mock exasperation, and everyone laughed, the terror of the previous moments dulled.

"I hate to say this," Argus grumbled through tight lips, "but I think we should spread out and *quickly* check each building before getting out of this place. I have a feeling there was more to our time here than that little show. Ren, Daijera, you two check out that tavern there. Ekko, Dalgis, and Elia, peek into those shops. Sora, Xezia, you're with me."

Chapter 2

Corruption

Ren

Ren's soul was haunted as he and Daijera toward the building Argus had indicated.

"What did you see?" she asked him softly.

He took a deep breath, still shaken by what he'd seen in the black muck. "I saw a child. It was crying, reaching for me." He paused, the shame of his life washing over him. "I don't know how I knew, but it was Princess Gya, the one I told you about. The one who was lost in Godfroy's insurrection. The one I abandoned."

"Ren, you were a child yourself, not even a knight yet. That goop was playing on your sense of guilt, but the truth is that that child was not your duty."

"She was, in my heart. I hear your logic, but I will never feel as though I did the right thing by abandoning the rightful rulers of Ironshield. What did you see?"

"I saw my mother," Daijera replied, a touch of ice in her voice. "It was more like a memory for me. She was telling me I was a fool to think I could carve out a life for myself away from the path she had chosen. Told me no one would ever see any lamia as more than a glorified whore." She spit the last word out as though it was poisonous. "But the truth is that I don't have any guilt over any decision I've ever made. Especially not leaving my mother and taking a different path. It was a bad memory, nothing more." Ren doubted that Daijera's feelings were

19

as simple as she made them seem, but now was not the time to push. They had a building to search.

Its second floor was whitewashed, the same as the others, but the lower level had rounded log halves adorning the wall every six feet. A shingle over the door identified it as the Wild Stag Tavern. When they were maybe 30 feet from the door, Daijera stopped suddenly and put a hand out to hold Ren back as well. She pointed to her ear, and Ren strained to listen. It took him a moment, but then he heard it, too: voices and faint music coming from within.

He gestured for Daijera to creep around back and see if there was another way in. She nodded and held up three fingers, indicating that he should give her three minutes of lead time. Then she darted off to the left of the building, out of sight.

Ren walked toward the building, then carefully positioned himself between the door and a window so that he could listen and not be seen by anyone who might look outside. Of course, someone might well have seen him already, but it seemed wise to exercise caution. The noises from within were exactly those one might expect from a tavern at mid-day: muffled conversation, the sound of a lute, occasional laughter, the soft *thunk* of tankards and plates landing on wooden tables.

He hazarded a quick peek through the window, and saw nothing out of the ordinary...had this been a typical tavern in a small town rather than an abandoned town square in the middle of the woods. He felt fairly certain three minutes had passed, so he reached for the door handle. It opened easily. He opted not to sheath his sword as one would normally do entering such an establishment, and he stepped inside.

There was nothing remarkable about the interior. The sunlight through the four small windows illuminated the room, revealing three long benched tables which would seat ten people each to the left, as well as four smaller tables with individual chairs to the right. Along the right-hand wall was a small bar, tended by a human male of about 40. Ren counted eight human patrons scattered at tables, and the lute player who was positioned between an empty fireplace and a door which presumably led to the kitchen.

The kitchen door eased open quietly and Daijera slipped into the main room. She spotted Ren, tilted her head toward the room she had just exited, and mouthed the word *empty*.

No one seemed to notice that the two of them had entered the room.

After surveying the room, Daijera shrugged at Ren and approached the lute player. Ren watched as she spoke to the musician, but received no reaction. Daijera looked back over her shoulder at Ren to make sure he was watching, then she raised her voice so it was loud enough that everyone in the room could easily hear.

"Do you mind if I play along with you? I'm a bit of a lute player myself." She pulled her own lute out of her pack and strummed along, harmonizing with the man beside her.

No one looked up.

Daijera slid her lute back into her bag and reached out to poke the man's shoulder. He hesitated, blinked, then went back to playing. She turned back to Ren and shouted across the room, "Well, they're not ghosts!"

Again, no one seemed to register her presence.

Confused, Ren clomped as loudly as he could across the room to where she was standing.

"What do you make of this?" he asked her.

"Bespelled?" she suggested.

Ren nodded. "That does seem to make the most sense. Perhaps, since they seem unaware of us, we should listen in on what they are saying. Perhaps they'll talk about what may be happening here."

"Good plan. Let's give it a few minutes, but then get out. I have a very bad feeling about this place."

They split up and worked their way around the room, meeting back by the bar.

"That guy over there," Daijera pointed, "is apparently a corn farmer. Did you happen to notice any fields as we were slogging through the woods after that idiot bird?"

"No, and although I heard some talking about families, we've already established that there are no houses around here. I do notice that everyone here is human. That seems a bit strange for Rosend, wouldn't you agree?"

"Very strange. I'm going to take a quick look behind the bar, then we're out of here."

"Daijera, I hardly think now is the time for..."

"Oh, skies above, Ren. I'm not looking for a drink. But if there's anything shady going on here, there will be clues behind the bar. Argus aside, barkeeps are the ultimate gatekeepers of shady business."

She stepped behind the bar and started rifling through the storage shelves. "Not much here out of the ordinary, but...hello...what's this? Ren, what do you make of these?" She held up a box of what appeared to be black iron coins with a skull on one side. She lifted one up to inspect it more closely.

"Um, Daijera, I'd suggest putting that back down," he said very evenly as the eyes of everyone in the room turned to stare at her and the coin in her hand.

"Why is...oh." She set the coin back in the box and returned the box to the shelf, and everyone returned to their activities, again oblivious to her presence. "Well, that wasn't creepy at all."

Ren opened the door. "Let's get back to the town square. Maybe someone else can..."

His words were cut off by a scream of agony in the distance, back the way they had come.

Elia

She didn't appreciate the fact that Argus had sent her off with Ekko and Dalgis. It wasn't that she didn't like Dalgis (she wasn't too sure how she felt about Ekko), it's just that those two were bonded, and Elia didn't like feeling like the odd-one-out. Especially not when she had just been traumatized by the voices of the dying soldiers she couldn't shield from the lava toad's attack.

You were supposed to protect us!

You're a deserter and a traitor!

You meant for us to die all along!

She knew the voices were being unfair, that they were some sort of trick, but when one wakes up covered in dead bodies, one tends to either repress those memories or go insane. And right now, she felt like it was the latter.

Still, she trudged along behind Ekko and Dalgis as they murmured together and approached the first storefront. Maybe she could scavenge some good supplies here; that is, if Ekko didn't get to them first.

"I'm afraid I'm too large to enter the premises," Dalgis announced, "but I shall stand watch over you. I believe it might be best if you stay together in case of trouble."

Great, Elia thought.

Ekko reached for the door handle of Burston's Provisions, and it opened easily.

"Maybe Squealer was just leading us to someplace with free supplies," she mused as the girls peered into the empty shop. Elia, though, wasn't convinced.

"I don't know; it seems a bit too easy, don't you think?"

Ekko shrugged. "Take the easy scores when you can; that's what I say. But only take what we can use. No point in carrying extra weight."

Elia scanned the shop while Ekko headed straight for the counter, no doubt to empty the money box. The room was small for a provisions shop, roughly 20 by 25 feet, if she had to hazard a guess. Dry goods appeared to be to the right. Several grain barrels, empty sacks, and a scale indicated that not everyone in this town had been farmers. Usually small quantities like these, only a pound or two at a time, were for daily purchases rather than the larger purchases people might make if they lived farther outside of town. She lifted the lid on one of the barrels. Flour, fairly finely milled. Another indication that this wasn't a rural settlement. Rural folks would have probably ground their own flour. She closed the lid, making note to tell Argus that whatever this place was once, this was only a tiny part of it.

Ekko had scooted into a back room, leaving Elia alone to search the store. She found a large satchel among some other textile-type items and began combing through the two sets of shelves and the large table in the center of the room. She gathered a few staples: candles, flint, a few pairs of gloves and socks, and some strips of dried meat which might come in handy if the hunting was no good. She came across some jars of honey, and pocketed two of them as an indulgence for later.

"Not too much in the back, though I did find a few things we could maybe sell when we get to a real town," Ekko reported. "Shall we move on to the next?"

Elia suspected Ekko had found a bit more than she disclosed, but it wasn't worth questioning her right now.

The next shop held bolts of fabric and some completed items of clothing. "These look a bit out-dated, don't they?" Elia asked.

Ekko turned a critical eye on the displays. "Now that you mention it, yes, they do. I only see older ladies wearing these." Ekko lifted a shoulder-wrap that secured to the waistline of skirts and trousers.

Another mysterious finding to report to Argus, Elia noted. She also noticed that these were town fashions, albeit ones that had fallen out of style, not the heavy fabrics one would expect farmers to purchase. Nor were they particularly useful travel clothes, so there wasn't anything worth shoving into the satchel.

The third and last shop, a stationers and bookstore, was the only one with a second story. "I'll check upstairs," Elia volunteered. "You look around here." And before Ekko could argue, Elia bolted up the wooden staircase opposite the door.

The second floor appeared to be a small living chamber, but unlike the stores they'd been in, this room was in a state of disarray. The small bed was unmade and rumpled, the desk was littered with books and papers, and the wardrobe had one of its doors flung open. Elia moved to the desk and began shuffling through the papers she found there.

Dearest Godfroy,

I hope that you are doing well. Things at home are most dull without you–

"Ex–excuse me," chirped a shaking, but stern voice from behind her, "it's–it's exceedingly impolite to go through someone's personal things." Elia jumped and spun around to see a girl of about 17 years old emerging from inside the wardrobe. "What do you think you are doing in my room?"

The girl had hair the color of clover honey and large, dark eyes. She was slight in build, but held a boot menacingly in one hand. Or at least she was trying to look menacing.

"What exactly do you think you're going to do with that?" Elia asked the girl. "As weapons go, that might be the worst I've ever seen."

"Well, it was either this or a winter scarf," the girl replied. "But you didn't answer my question."

"I didn't think anyone was here."

"That's no excuse to go into someone's private room."

"You misunderstand. I didn't think there was anyone *in the whole town*. You're the first person I've seen. I'm Elia. What's your name?"

"My name is Imogen. I haven't seen anyone today, actually. Well, that's not precisely true. There are people in the Wild Stag, but they ignored me when I went in there."

"Just today, you said?" Elia asked. She'd been working on a theory that somehow this town was frozen in time, but if Imogen was right, then there had to be some other explanation for the empty streets and out-of-style clothes.

"I think so. I don't really have a good sense of time. I can't remember what I did a week ago, or a year ago. I only remember going to sleep yesterday and waking up today. And today everything was pretty quiet until your group arrived. I saw you out the window."

"Did we interrupt you as you were writing a letter to the king of Ironshield?" Elia tried to keep all tone of disapproval out of her voice.

"King? Good heavens, no. What king would want anything to do with me? I was writing to my brother. He's gone to Ironshield City to become a wizard. There is a college there."

"Godfroy is a very unusual name. Was he named after the king?"

"Where is there a king named Godfroy?"

Ekko popped her head into the room. "Elia, did you find...oh, I guess you did. Hello!"

"Hello. Why are you people here? Where has everyone else gone?" Imogen was becoming agitated, wringing the boot in her hands. "I don't feel very well."

"I'm sorry we've upset you, Imogen," Elia began, "but we think something bad might have happened here. I think it might be wise if you were to come with us so we can keep you safe."

"With you and that fearsome beast?"

"Fearsome...oh, Dalgis? He isn't fearful at all," Ekko replied cheerfully. "Unless you are a very bad person. Then he is most frightening, I should think."

"I promise you will be safe with us, Imogen. We're just trying to figure out what's going on, and there are some indications that this town is...less than secure."

"Well, alright," Imogen said, resigned. She dropped the boot. "Maybe I'll just come with you until we get to another town. Then

I'll try and get in touch with my brother. Our parents are dead, you see. The Bronswell family lets me live here if I manage their store downstairs, and..."

From outside, an anguished cry rent the air. The three girls stared at each other, then rushed down the stairs to find Dalgis.

Xezia

"Argus, could I have a few words with my colleague here before we follow you?" Sora glared at Xezia, her hands on her hips.

The wizard raised an eyebrow, then walked off in the direction of the building they were to investigate, stopped at a respectful distance, and turned his back to her.

"Sora..." Xezia began.

"Shut up and don't interrupt me," she snapped. "I have never needed protection from anyone in my entire life, Xezia..."

"Sora, just listen..."

"I said don't interrupt, and I meant it. You *will* listen to what I have to say." Xezia snapped his mouth shut, but forced himself not to look away, silently challenging her rage. She took a step toward him. "I can take care of myself, and you know it. Since the day we met, there are two things that were unquestionably true." Her voice and expression softened as she looked at him. "The first is that, even though you know I'm capable, your instinct is to step between me and danger. The second is that you have this darkness within you, and you fight it every single day. You don't always win, but you fight."

His eyes widened, and he was suddenly very unsure about where she was going with this.

"Do you know what those things together prove, Xezia?" she continued, pressing her hand against his chest. "They prove that, even though I'm sure you'd deny it, you have deep nobility within you. You may not always be honest, maybe not even good, but at your core, you are noble."

Xezia opened his mouth to say something, but no words would come, so he closed it again. He felt stripped of his defenses, completely unprepared to respond. Panic, relief, and joy battled within him. Her hand, warm against his heart, cracked something within him, and the feelings leaking out were ones he didn't know how to feel.

"You must never stop fighting, Xezia. Protect that part of you as fiercely as you protect me." She closed her fist, wadding up his shirt front, and pulled him toward her into a rough kiss.

THE KISS ONLY LASTED a couple of seconds, but when she pulled away, grinned and stomped after Argus, Xezia was unable to follow. The feeling of her lips on his had created heat within him, yes, but that was to be expected. What surprised him was not the heat; it was the *warmth* he felt. For the first time he could remember, he felt *connected* to someone. And he realized, as he watched her walk away, that he would do anything for her, anything to protect that connection.

He followed slowly, but his mind was spinning. To hell with this quest. To hell with the Black Moon. When they made it back to civilization, he would suggest to her that they disappear, that they go find a seaside town where she could get a boat and charter passengers, shipments, whatever she wanted. That would make her happy, to be back by the sea. And he would...well, he would do *something* for a living. He could figure that out later.

He caught up with the two of them, and Argus cast a glance back at him. "What's wrong with you?" he asked.

Xezia realized that he was grinning. Really grinning.

"Don't pay any attention to him," Sora quipped. "He's an idiot." But she shot him a quick wink over her shoulder, and he found himself wanting to throw his arms around her and never let go.

The structure in front of them looked as though it had once been a place of worship, though it had been vandalized and damaged, unlike the other buildings in town. It was a single-story building, rectangular in shape, roughly the size of a small barn. The wooden door, covered with burn marks like they'd seen on the signpost, had been ripped from its hinges and lay several feet away. The whitewashed exterior showed clear signs that it had been attacked with hammers and other tools.

Before they entered, Argus spun on Xezia.

"Alright, Xezia, before we take one more step, you're going to need to level with me. What is going on with you and that black substance?"

"Wha...what?" Xezia's attention was ripped away from the image of Sora coiling rope on the deck of a small sailing vessel. "What do you mean?"

"Don't play dumb; it doesn't suit you. This is the third time I've seen you speak a language none of us can identify, including you. I saw enough of the Book of Order to recognize that some of the sounds you made are similar to what's in there. And then there's that." He pointed at Xezia's hand, where he had been bitten by the small flying creature weeks before. The finger where he'd been bitten was almost entirely black, and dark spiderwebby veins spread across the entire hand. "You want to tell me that it's pure coincidence that we keep coming across this gelatinous darkness, and a similar-looking gunk is spreading through your hand from a bite you received in an attack where *you* were clearly the target? The rest of us are risking our necks in this quest, but it's considerably more dangerous if there's something going on here that you're hiding from us."

"Whatever is going on with Xexia, it doesn't have anything to do with anyone else," Sora retorted.

"It's okay, Sora," Xezia thought his heart might actually burst as she stepped to his defense. "You're right, Argus, there is a connection, but I don't know what it is. I don't know why I know that language. I don't know why this darkness is targeting me. But if I feel like I'm putting the rest of you at risk, you have my word that I'll leave the party. Whatever is happening to me isn't my doing."

Argus regarded him through narrowed eyes. "And whatever this is, it's not interfering with your decision-making?"

"Not at this point, no. I swear I won't endanger anyone." He snuck a glance at Sora, and the look in her eyes sent a warm shiver through his slender frame.

Argus nodded solemnly and directed a pointed look at the holy symbol around the mage's neck. "I'll hold you to that." And then he turned on his heel and stepped through the ruined doorway.

If the outside of the temple looked damaged, the inside of the temple looked like a battle zone. It appeared that six shrines had been housed here, three on each wall, but they had been smashed and desecrated. Alcoves with images of the six deities and spaces for gifts from worshippers were blackened and burned, smeared with what looked like dried blood and livestock manure.

Argus knelt to examine some of the burn patterns around the doorway, and Sora moved to the second alcove on the left, which appeared to have once represented Hoshkn. She took out her flask and began trying to clean the shattered statuette.

"What happened here?" Xezia wondered aloud, surveying the damage and walking toward the space where Epi's followers would have come.

A deep and distorted chuckle echoed throughout the temple.

Xezia spun around, searching for the origin of the sound. Argus leapt up and peered out the door, and Sora whipped out her short sword, still gripping the stone idol in her other hand.

The laughter grew louder and more sinister, and the air began to vibrate. There was a cry from Argus as an invisible force blew him through the entryway and out of the temple. He tried to rush back in, but the force now blocked the door, denying him access.

"What...?" The fear in Sora's voice caused Xezia's heart to thud against his ribs. Black ooze had begun seeping through the cracks in the wooden floor, and Sora was backing into Hoshkn's alcove to try and escape it, but no part of the floor appeared to be safe.

"No!" Xezia shouted, the terror of his vision in the Deep Woods coming back to him. "Sora, you have to get out of here!"

"I can't! There's nowhere to go!" The goop enveloped her feet and began creeping up her legs, and the walls, at an alarming rate.

Xezia looked down at his own feet, which were also covered, though the muck didn't appear to be trying to envelop him.

"Xezia! Help! I can't move!" There was panic in her voice now, and in the split second he had looked away, the blackness had advanced to her waist.

He tried to move toward her, but his feet were stuck to the ground like stone. The laughter reached a fevered pitch.

"Leave her alone!" he cried. "I don't know who you are, but it's me you're after, not her!"

Do you not know who I am? How disappointing. I gave you more credit for cleverness.

The suspicions and fears that had followed him since childhood pounded in his brain.

Say my name, Xezia.

"Ipthel. Please. Spare her. Do what you want with me. Spare Sora."

She clutched the statue of Hoshkn to her chest as the darkness covered her torso. "Fight, Xezia. Always fight." Her voice was defiant, even as tears escaped her eyes. A second later, and she looked like a statue made of onyx.

"No," Xezia whispered. "Not her. Anyone but her."

I believe I will hold onto her for the moment, my lad. Lest your rebellious nature get the better of you.

"She's not dead?" Xezia's heart fluttered with hope.

Not currently, no. I imagine it's up to you if that remains the case.

"What do you want from me?"

I want you to stop this charade. I claimed you that night in the village. Do you truly believe it was an accident that those crazed fools spared you alone?

"Those crazed fools were *your* followers!"

Fools, the lot of them. Incapable of fulfilling my true vision. The only thing they knew how to do was destroy. What good is a ruined world? No good to me, I assure you. My followers here started to understand that, but even they gave in to their primal instincts. Mortals always do, it seems, but you can put an end to all that.

"Me? Why me?"

Because, as I said, you have a rare cleverness. You can understand what I truly am. You can make things different.

"What you truly are? You're the God of Corruption!" Xezia was dimly aware of Argus shouting, presumably still trying to get back in.

Ugh, don't be so simple. Mortals always seem to see things as one or the other. Life and Death. Order and Chaos. Purity and Corruption. But the truth is that all those things are intricately connected and interdependent. You are capable of seeing a bigger picture. Agree to serve me, and I will show you how we can bring balance back to a world torn asunder.

Xezia stared at the blackened image of Sora. "I will fight. Every day I will fight."

A sigh echoed through the room, much like an adult trying to reason with an obstinate child.

Have it your way. I will hold onto her until you change your mind. And you will, I assure you.

In a blink, the black ooze receded, leaving Xezia alone.

Gone. She was gone.

He felt as though his soul had been ripped from his body, and the grief inside him erupted in a wail of despair that carried within it a lifetime of loneliness and emptiness.

Chapter 3

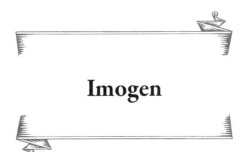

Imogen

Argus

He couldn't hear what was happening, but he saw it all.

As soon as the invisible barrier divided them, Argus had tried everything he could to break through it.

He'd used fire magic.

He'd used lightning magic.

He'd used ice magic.

Then he'd thrown a rock.

Nothing worked.

The wizard watched the muck burble out from the cracks in the stone, and he watched as Xezia and Sora became stuck. He watched Xezia shout into the air as the darkness enveloped his friend. Then Argus watched in helpless horror as the black goo sucked itself back into the floor, taking any trace of Sora with it. Then the barrier had disappeared with the last of the ooze, and Xezia sunk to the ground like a wet shirt slipping off the clothesline. Then he threw his head back and let out a howl of anguish that actually made Argus feel genuine pity toward the man he had deemed too shifty to ever be trusted.

"Xezia," Argus rushed to the mage's side. "Xezia, what happened?"

"Gone. She's gone. He took her."

"Who took her?"

"Ipthel. He wants something from me, and if I don't give it to him, he'll kill her."

Ipthel? The Deity of Corruption? Why would he be making a personal appearance here? Had they incurred his ire by possessing the Book of Order? Argus's mind began whirring with questions, theories, and suppositions, but he knew now was not the time to talk through them.

He crouched down and put his hand on Xezia's shoulder. "So she's alive?"

"He says so."

"What does he want in exchange for her life?"

"I don't know exactly. He just said for me to serve him." Xezia's arms hung limply at his sides, palms up, the blackened veins in his hand a stark reminder of Ipthel's evil touch.

"That's not an option, of course, but we have time to figure something out if she's still alive. Hope isn't lost." Argus's attention was drawn to Xezia's hand. "It's time you leveled with me so I can try to help you, son. How long has Ipthel been after you?"

Xezia shook his head and looked up at Argus forlornly. "I don't know. Maybe my whole life. I...he...followers of Ipthel destroyed my village, but left me alive. I was eight. There were bodies everywhere. My family, my friends...everyone. But the cultists ignored me like I was a piece of furniture. When they left, I wandered in shock for days, and this strange old priest of Epi found me. He started to train me. I prayed to Epi every night, sometimes for hours at a time. I promised to wipe those bastards off the land and make it pure. I promised I would avenge her. Every night I promised her." His eyes were pleading, as if Argus could grant him some sort of absolution.

"And this priest, that's how he taught you to pray to Epi?"

"He told me the cultists were an affront to Her purity. That they were the antithesis of everything Epi stands for."

"He spoke true. But did he tell you to pray for vengeance, Xezia?'

"Not precisely. But he didn't tell me not to." Xezia wiped the tears from his cheek with his sleeve and his hardened expression returned, a gesture that reminded Argus vaguely of the way a child might do if he didn't want to appear weak in front of an adult. "What does it matter what the old fool told me or didn't tell me? Obviously Epi wasn't listening!"

"Hold now, Xezia. I understand your rage, truly. I have, in all my study of the gods, never heard of Epi endorsing vengeance of any kind. I don't believe that is a prayer she would answer. But that doesn't mean she didn't hear you. I would submit to you that she may be watching and waiting for you to follow her according to her doctrines, not your own." Argus tried to say this gently, but the criticism was important. He felt as though the younger man was at a great moral crossroads.

"What are you trying to say, Argus?"

"I'm saying that Ipthel may have had his eye on you your whole life, to your point. I'm saying that if that's true, maybe he found a way to ensure you were found by someone who couldn't train you properly in Epi's ways. So maybe you thought you were serving her, but..."

"Don't even say it!" Xezia interrupted. His voice was harsh, but his eyes betrayed his doubts.

"Xezia, listen, if Sora is alive, then we certainly must try to save her if we can. Drawing yourself closer to Epi may be the only way to accomplish that."

"Or I could just give that bastard what he wants."

"You could. But that probably wouldn't end well. And it assumes he'd keep his end of the bargain. Ipthel isn't known for straight dealing." Argus stood and reached out a hand to Xezia to help him stand. The gesture seemed to startle the mage, as though it reminded him of something.

"You might be right, Argus," Xezia said, taking the wizard's hand and pulling himself up. "But I think I'll need to keep communication open with him while I search for a way to commune with Epi. I have always had trouble doing that, and now I think I know why. But I'm going to have to play both sides so I don't risk him taking out his wrath on Sora."

"You can't be certain he hasn't already done so, you know."

"I'm not an imbecile, Argus. I know that. But I can't take the chance. And you can't tell the others about this, at least not the part about Ipthel trying to get me into his service. I told you I won't endanger anyone, and I won't. I swear it. I swear on the lives of my entire village."

"I think it would mean more if you swore on your own."

"Fine, then. I swear on my own life. I'll leave the group and strike out on my own before I intentionally put anyone in any peril. But you can't tell them. My best chance to reach Epi is to stick with this quest, this group. If they knew, they might cast me out. Please, Argus."

Argus ground his teeth in frustration, certain that he would regret this decision. "Very well, Xezia. I'll keep your secret for the moment, but the second I suspect you of turning on us..."

"I know, I know. But I won't. You have my word."

Argus made a conscious effort not to snort in derision at that. "Alright then. For now."

Xezia nodded solemnly, and Argus could almost hear the gears of the young man's mind turning as he tried to figure out how to save his friend. Xezia ran his tongue along the inside of his cheek and his gaze wandered off as he pondered. For just an instant, Argus was certain he caught the slightest glint in Xezia's eye.

Yes, he was definitely going to regret this. He could feel it in his bones.

Dalgis

He wasn't sure what to do. Should he run toward the sound of the wail that had torn the quiet of the town, or should he stay and guard the girls? A clattering from within the store solved his inner conflict, but when Elia and Ekko returned with a third girl in tow, he was filled with confusion again.

"I regret I'm not quite sure what to do. I am pleased that you are all safe and sound...and hello, young lady. My name is Dalgis...but who do you suppose made that horrible sound?"

"I don't know, but it has to be one of us, right?" Elia worried. "Which way did it come from?"

"Across the square that way," he answered. "Stay close to me; I shan't let you come to harm!" He puffed up his frill and rose to his full height of nearly 11 feet. The new girl squeaked and hid behind Elia, a difficult task, since Elia was less than half Dalgis's height.

"Dalgis won't hurt you, Imogen," Ekko reassured her. "Not unless you try to hurt one of us."

Imogen nodded, but then threw her hands over her mouth in alarm. Dalgis and Ekko looked around in concern.

"I almost forgot all my things!" Imogen gasped, and then ran back inside.

"Great skies," Ekko grumbled, "I hardly think that was worth her reaction. I guess we'd better wait for her, though; I don't want her running off somewhere. Something weird is going on here, and she's our best bet at figuring out exactly what."

From the direction of the tavern, Daijera and Ren appeared, also clearly headed cautiously toward the sound they had all heard. Dalgis, worried that one of his friends might be in trouble, started inching his way in the same direction.

The girl reappeared a moment later with a small satchel slung over her shoulder. "I really don't have that many things," she said apologetically, "but there were a few possessions I wouldn't want to leave behind."

"Marvelous, then, we're all set. Let us not tarry any longer. Someone might be in grave danger!" He began trotting toward the center of town, trusting that the girls would follow.

He caught up with Ren and Daijera at the fountain.

"Dalgis," Ren began, "do you have any idea whose voice that was?"

"I can't be completely certain, but it rather sounded like...Xezia?" The mage was solemnly following behind Argus as they emerged from the temple. Xezia's shoulders were slumped, his eyes downcast. "Argus, Xezia, where's Sora?"

Argus raised his eyes to Dalgis and shook his head sadly. Xezia turn his head away, looking back from whence they'd come. "She's been taken...by Ipthel," he mumbled, his voice cracking.

Everyone fell silent, staring at the two men. Neither volunteered any additional information.

"I'm terribly sorry to push, as I'm sure this is a very difficult time for you, but did you say *Ipthel*? He was here? And when you say *taken*, do you mean stolen, or..." Dalgis couldn't bring himself to say the words. He felt a lump in his throat at the thought of the sun elf's death.

Xezia didn't respond, but after a moment, Argus replied, "I can't say for sure, Dalgis, but I fear the worst. And yes, He was here. It appears that His evil hand has been on this town for some time."

"Ipthel's worshippers destroyed the community temple," came Imogen's hesitant voice. The rest of the party started, not having noticed her until that moment. "I don't remember when that was, though. But I know it happened a while ago."

"And who is this?" Ren asked, his voice carefully emotionless.

"This is Imogen," Elia responded. "She is from...here...this town. Where exactly are we, Imogen? The sign at the edge of town was destroyed."

"Emberell. Our village is called Emberell. I remember that!" She seemed very proud. Argus's eyebrows twitched slightly, but he said nothing.

"Okay, good," Elia continued, "and anyway, since she appears to be the only person here, I thought she'd better come with us."

Daijera had been studying Imogen closely. "Oh, there are other people here, but they're not like her. They're, um, well, there's something not right about them. Let's leave it at that for the time being." Ren nodded in agreement. "I think it would be a good idea for us to get out of this town immediately." She walked over to Xezia and laid her hand on his sleeve. He shook his head and pulled his arm away, but then mumbled something that sounded like *thank you* as an afterthought.

"Right then," announced Dalgis, "let's put some distance between us and this accursed place. I swear, we will find a way to avenge our fallen compatriot!"

The group started walking slowly back toward the barn and the edge of the village.

"I say, Argus," Dalgis muttered to the wizard, "do you know something about this town? You seemed to react ever so slightly when young Imogen mentioned its name."

"The name was familiar," he admitted, "but the Emberell I know of is in Ironshield, not Rosend. The one in Ironshield was, I believe, the birthplace of the Blood King."

A cry from the front of the group cut off Dalgis's reply.

"Wha– what's happening to me?" It was Imogen's voice. She was staring at her hands in horror.

Her fair skin was growing paler and her palms were stained black. She turned around to look at her new friends, and the now-familiar black substance was leaking from her ears, nose, and eyes. She began to cry and tremble in fear.

"Come back home, Imogen. You're safe here. You're protected here. Come home."

They spun around to find a group of about twenty people staring at them with empty eyes. They spoke with one voice, a discordant chorus.

Daijera let out a hissing sound. "It's the people from the tavern," she warned.

Her chest heaving, Imogen was slipping into hysteria. "No! What's happening? Somebody help me!" She turned her pleading eyes to Dalgis, then to Argus. "Are they doing this to me?"

"You can't leave, Imogen. Stay with us." The tavern crowd continued their advance, shuffling down the street toward the barn.

"Good gracious!" Dalgis cried. "Are they..." As the mob approached, their appearance, which had been mostly normal except for their blankness, began to shift and change, as Imogen's had. Their human eyes had become leaky, inky black holes, and goopy drool dribbled down their chins.

Imogen shrieked. "No! I'm not like you! I'm not!" She inched closer to the signpost, and though her eyes remained brown, the skin around them thinned, revealing a roadmap of dark veins underneath.

"Imogen," Argus said softly, laying his hand on her shoulder to stop her movement, "I know you still feel like yourself, but it's clear that you are transforming as you get farther away from your home. I'm not sure what's happening here, but I feel confident that you are unable to leave."

"I'm not like them," she whimpered, ebony rivulets tracing their way down her cheeks. "I don't want to stay here with them. I'm frightened."

"My dear girl," Dalgis tried to sound soothing, but there was no comforting away the tragedy before him, "the only way you can survive is to stay."

"I can't...I can't stay here...they're not human." She looked at her stained hands. "I'm not human either, am I?"

"I can't be certain what you are, I'm afraid," Argus said sadly.

The town residents had stopped moving when she did. She stared at them, then back at her own arms, now ashen and slick with ichor. Suddenly, she raised her head, clarity and resolve in her eyes. An inhuman growl rose from the mob.

"You will DIE!" It wasn't clear if that was a threat or a warning.

"I'm already dead!" she shouted at them. Then she turned back to Elia. "Thank you for trying to help me and be my friend." She reached into her satchel. "Please, if you ever go to Ironshield City, go to the wizard college and find my brother. Give him this, and tell him I loved him till the very last. Tell him I was brave!" She pressed a book into Elia's hands and then sprinted for the signpost.

THE MOB HOWLED IN UNISON and shot forward in a lumbering run.

"Time to go!" Daijera announced, and started running after Imogen. The rest of the group followed suit.

Each step closer to the freedom of the forest intensified Imogen's deterioration. When she collapsed against the post, her skin had begun to melt like wax, exposing bone underneath. She turned her eyes toward Elia once more as she rolled herself into the green grass of the forest. What was left of her shuddered into a puddle of blackness, leaving only her clothes and her skeleton behind.

The sounds of the running crowd ceased. Dalgis shot a quick look behind him as the citizens turned gelatinous and sunk into the cobblestones like tar, leaving no trace of their existence behind.

He turned to find Elia clutching a book of children's stories to her chest, her eyes filled with tears. He could tell she fought not to let them fall.

One by one, the rest of the party stepped off of the stone road and into the woods. Once he was certain that everyone was safe, Dalgis stepped off the path to join them.

"*SQUEEEEEAL!*" shrieked the bird as the signpost and the rest of the village square faded into nothing, leaving only the dense forest behind. Squealer flapped into a nearby tree and commenced to preen his wings.

"Okay, what in the name of the Six just happened?" shouted Ekko.

"If I'm adding up the evidence correctly," Argus replied through gritted teeth, "I believe that we just met some twisted form of King Godfroy's sister."

"How is that possible?"

"I suspect that will take me a bit longer to figure out. But with the exception of the element of time, everything else seems to lean in that direction. And I'm afraid we have one more task to take care of before we can move on."

No one spoke as Argus and Xezia built a magical pyre that burned Imogen's bones, but everyone was thinking about the timid girl who, in her final and desperate act, had found the courage to be free.

Chapter 4

Friendly Faces

Argus

He missed his family.

He felt the homesickness all the time, of course, but seeing two people die in the space of an hour brought things into perspective. Well, maybe they weren't deaths in the literal sense, but despite Xezia's protestations to the contrary, Argus suspected Sora was either dead or something worse. And technically, Imogen had already been dead, but she hadn't known it, so essentially it was like witnessing her demise.

Regardless of the definitional debates about whether they were deaths or not, the events of Emberell had left Argus wanting to wrap his arms around his family and not let go. Unfortunately, he had to finish what he'd started here, because someone had to keep the shifty people away from the Holy Books. So that meant he couldn't go home. Not yet.

Verwoerd was roughly two day's journey from the mysterious disappearing village, as long as the weather held out and they didn't run into any problems. The proprietor at the Silver Branch Inn was an old friend; his father had worked as a bartender for Argus's father decades ago. Argus and Colvyn had been thick as thieves as children, but when Godfroy came into power, the Blood King had advised any non-human races that a change in residence was their only escape; Ironshield would be purified by blood and fire if they didn't choose to go on their own. So Colvyn and his family, who were sun elves with a bit of storm elf blood somewhere in their veins, had pulled up roots and gone back toward the land of their ancestors.

Two days of mild weather meant easy travel, and Argus was grateful for it. "It won't be long now," Argus announced to the group. "These farms mark the southern edge of Verwoerd. He found himself feeling lighter than he had in a couple of weeks. Colvyn might not be family, but he was a familiar and friendly face, which was something Argus found himself anticipating with something bordering on excitement.

Verwoerd was a town of some size, and as they walked past the farms, people working the fields would occasionally look up and wave, though they were strangers. Argus waved back and smiled each time. This was how life should be. Simple. Peaceful. People did their part to keep the community strong, and generally stayed out of trouble. Life didn't have to be so complicated.

"I'd almost forgotten what civilization looked like," Ekko chuckled as they approached the wall that ringed the central part of the town. "How come there's no one watching the gates? Aren't they worried about Ironshield raiding parties?"

"Make no mistake, their town militia is prepared for such things. The outer wall of the city here is actually more like a long tube that rings the interior part of Verwoerd. There are archers within the walls, patrolling and watching for danger." Argus pointed to the arrow slits camouflaged into the stonework as they passed through the massive stone archway and into the city proper. The lower spikes of an iron portcullis peeked out from the ceiling as well. "There are also warning stations with bell towers spread all over the area, so if a citizen sees a war party, they head for one of those and warn everyone."

"That seems efficient," she nodded in approval.

"It is. But the townsfolk here refuse to make any other concessions beyond that. They are a wonderfully stubborn people who refuse to live in fear of the Blood King."

Ekko nodded again, a slight smile teasing the corners of her mouth. Argus hoped it was because she respected the townsfolk's spirit, and not because she was planning to test it.

The wide streets of the town were bustling with life. Horse or donkey-drawn carts clattered down the hard-packed dirt of the road, and pedestrians strolled along either side, chatting and carrying purchases. Most of the residents appeared to have some amount of elvish blood, if their pointed ears were any indication, but there were also humans, dwarves, and a few other odd races scattered through the streets. The mixed heritage of the party was a reflection of the town's population, although Dalgis still garnered a few raised eyebrows and curious stares.

"Ah, there, see that statue of the dragon on the next corner? We'll be turning left there. The Silver Branch is a couple of storefronts down on the right."

The front of the inn was just as he remembered it. The framing was wooden, but flat stones had been mortared in between the support beams to try and insulate from the winter cold and also as a hedge against the spread of fire, should one break out. The glass windows were divided into six sections each, ostensibly to increase the strength of the window, but also to pay homage to the six deities. Most people had forgotten that last part, but Argus had learned it in his studies and found it fascinating.

The number six was used repeatedly in Verwoerd's town planning. Most frontages had six windows (usually three upstairs and three downstairs, though not always), and most of the in-town dwellings had six units. Even the inn complied with the law of six: there were six rooms for guests on each of two upstairs stories, and there were two sets of six stables in the back. Even the sign hanging above the door showed a tree with six silver arms stretching toward the sky, each with six leaves. Argus found all the symmetry comfortable and relaxing.

"Let me check inside to make sure Colvyn has enough lodging for all of us," Argus said to the group. "I won't be but a few moments." He stepped inside and let his eyes adjust to the dimness of the inside. Several patrons took up tables in the tavern side of the main room, holding the full attention of the barkeep with their orders and noisy banter, so Argus stepped up to the registration desk and rang the bell that sat next to the guestbook on the counter.

"Oh, tinkle-tinkle! I'm coming!" came a voice from the small office behind a wall of what looked like mailbox cubbies. There was a grunt, some shuffling, and then an elderly elf toddled out of the doorway. She wore a bright blue tunic with the Silver Branch logo embroidered across the front. "Well, as I live and breathe! Is this Argus Chasmag I see before me, or are my ancient eyes playing tricks?"

A rare smile erupted across the wizard's face. "Well met, *ora-ini*," he greeted the woman with the common elvish term for *grandmother*. Yana Portuna was Colvyn's maternal grandmother, and the matriarch of his household. "I'm most pleased to see you."

"Surprised I'm not in a knitting circle with Hoshkn, you mean." She grinned and took his hand in hers, patting it as one might do with a puppy. "It is good to see you, my boy. How is Sier?"

"She is well, *ora-ini*."

"And the twins?"

"Growing stronger everyday."

"As it should be. Will you be staying with us?"

"Yes, indeed, if you have the space. I'm with a sizable party."

"How many rooms then?" she asked, squinting at the guestbook.

"Six rooms and a large stable pen."

"Well, you came at a good time. I can give you the whole third floor. A couple of days ago, I'm not sure we coulda fit you in. You sign the book here, boy, and I'll go let Colvyn know you're here. He'll be right thrilled."

"Thank you, *ora-ini*."

"Such a good boy." She patted his hand one more time and walked back into the office. Argus heard a door open and close, and reasoned that Colvyn was probably in the stable yard somewhere. He signed the book and then poked his head back out.

"They have sufficient room. Come on in if you wish."

"I'll stay with Dalgis until they can get his stall set up," Ekko volunteered.

Dalgis flashed her a toothy grin. "That's most considerate of you, young Ekko."

The rest of the party stepped inside just as Colvyn and his grandmother returned. "Ah, Argus! I'm glad you made it! Sier's delivery came two days ago, so I knew you'd make it here eventually." He pulled Argus into a brotherly hug and slapped his back soundly. "This is quite a crew you have traveling with you, friend!"

"You don't know the half of it," Argus muttered, but his smirk betrayed his surly remark.

"Let me get your things so you can get settled. Hold on." Colvyn stepped back into the office and returned a moment later with a large basket in his arms. "Sier included some fairly specific instructions with your supplies..." he began.

"I'd expect as much."

"She was very specific about not tipping the box of inks, so we've been careful. Can't be sure about the courier, though. Also, she seems to have baked you some of those dandelion cookies, if I'm any judge of the smell, and I'll be expecting one of them as payment."

Argus chuckled and nodded. "Again, I'd expect as much."

"And finally, there's this fella..." He gingerly lifted a cage from the basket. Inside the cage was a very grumpy looking lizard. "I know we were supposed to give Stig here mealworms, but he was being petulant and wouldn't eat what Sier sent. So I had the kids run around and catch him some moths. He looked a bit put out, but he did eat them."

"*Stig?*" Argus stared at the bright blue and green lizard, who cocked his head in response.

Xezia spoke up. "Argus, did your wife send your pet? Or is that some poor fool you transfigured at some point?"

"No, he's just a lizard," Argus replied, trying to seem nonchalant. He took the cage from Colvyn and opened the door.

Stig leapt onto Argus's cuff, up his sleeve, and into his hood. Then he hissed and promptly went to sleep.

"Well, he certainly seems happy to see you, old friend. How old is that damn thing anyway? He looks just like he did last time you came through. Must be all the mealworms, right? Anyway, here are your keys. The third floor is yours, and I've asked my stablehand to take down the boards dividing two of our stables to accommodate your request for a large stall. Why don't you all get settled and then come down to dinner and we'll have a chat?"

"We'll do that, thank you, Colvyn."

Everyone tromped up the wooden stairs and their soft chatter faded as they made their way to the third floor. Argus smiled and gave his friend a brief nod as he took possession of the basket of supplies. After a moment, he followed the others, listening to soft hissy snoring sounds coming from inside his hood.

Daijera

She wondered if anyone else had noticed the partially-hooded figure who hadn't taken their eyes off of them since they entered the Silver Branch Inn. Xezia had hardly said a word since Emberell, and no one else seemed to have the sense to be suspicious of random people in taverns.

AFTER DROPPING HER bag in her room, she hustled back down to the tavern, only to find the stranger's table empty. Maybe it was nothing; maybe she was being paranoid. But she doubted it. Her instincts were rarely wrong.

"Well, now, that didn't take you long, dearie. Fancy lady like you? I expected you'd be bathing for at least three quarters of an hour." The elven matriarch was perched back at the registration desk, eyeing Daijera somewhat suspiciously.

"What? Oh," she laughed heartily at the old woman's judgemental tone, "I definitely have some freshening up to do. I just thought I saw someone I knew, and I was coming back down to check. That sand elf that was sitting over there...was his name Osric?"

The lady's graying brows knitted together in disapproval. "Nope, 'fraid not. That there was a shady character named Dunach. He comes in here from time to time, sips his ale and watches the folks who are checking in. Always sits in that same seat in the corner, prob'ly so no one can sneak up behind him. I always think he's lookin' at who might be good to rob, but so far no one's reported anything being stolen, so I got no grounds to kick him out."

"Thanks for the warning...I'm sorry, I don't think we've been properly introduced. I'm Daijera."

"My proper name is Yana, but most everyone calls me *ona*. I s'pose you can call me that, too."

Daijera noted that she had left off the suffix of *ini*, which was an elven designation of affection and respect. "*Ona* it is then. Thank you." She smiled brightly, but the elf just crossed her arm and clucked her tongue.

"I got a pretty good sense of people, Miss Daijera, and I suspect you've got a very different face sometimes than the one I'm seeing."

Taken aback, Daijera paused for a moment and then replied, "Well, I suppose you're more astute than most. I may look human, but..." she dropped her glamour and let her true appearance show through, "I'm actually a lamia. I don't advertise the fact because men make certain–assumptions–when they come across one of my kind."

"Uh-huh," Ona clucked again. "Somehow I think there's more to it, but that does explain a bit. Word of advice: don't go lookin' for that sketchy character. He radiates trouble and I don't want any trouble in my grandson's place."

"I wouldn't want to cause any kind of trouble, especially not for a friend of Argus's."

The woman seemed satisfied with that response and nodded curtly. Daijera decided that a bath sounded pretty good after all. She needed to wash off all those dirty looks.

An hour later, the group was gathered at a large tavern table, consuming copious quantities of rabbit stew. Ekko had taken a pot of it out to Dalgis, and now seemed to be consuming nearly as much as he had. She licked her lips, not wasting a single oily drop.

"I'll take that as a compliment, Miss Ekko," smiled Colvyn.

"As well you should. Rabbit is my favorite, and people nearly always overcook it. But this is perfect," she beamed.

"I'm pleased you're enjoying it. But back to what I was saying, I don't know of any large temples to Hohn near here. I mean, there is a shrine, and I suppose it's a good-sized one, but nothing like what you're asking about."

Xezia sighed heavily and poked at his stew.

"Might there be any storm elves in town?" Elia asked innocently, evoking a hearty chortle from Colvyn

"I'm about as much storm elf as you'll find in a town like this, and my storm blood is three generations back."

"You should send them to ask Moraia," *Ona* said as she dropped off a plate of warm bread. Daijera smiled in spite of herself. She admired the completely unabashed way in which the old lady had been eavesdropping.

"Moraia? Oh, yes...she may indeed have some information."

"Who's Moraia?" asked Argus.

"Moraia is, well, I'm not sure what she is exactly. But she does have an impressive flower booth at the mid-week market sometimes."

"Wouldn't that make her a farmer?" Ekko quipped between bites of bread.

"Normally, yes, but there's no flower farms near here, and some of what she brings isn't exactly local. There are rumors that she gets her stock by magical means."

"Magical?" Daijera leaned in, her interest piqued.

"Well, yes. She does wear an amulet with Hohn's symbol on it, too, which is probably why *ona-ini* suggested you speak with her."

"Is she a priestess?" Argus wondered.

"If she is, she sure doesn't preach much. She just shows up, sells flowers, talks to people, and then disappears until the next market day. Or not. Sometimes she's there and sometimes she isn't. No one knows where she lives as far as I'm aware."

Ona grunted from across the room, though whether it was in agreement or disagreement was hard to say.

"What about Ironshield?" asked Argus. "Have there been any raiding parties around here lately? Any trouble?"

"Ach, nothing we can't handle," Colvyn replied, disdain in his voice. "They sometimes pick around the outskirts of town, but it doesn't do them much good around here. Old man Creely saw them sniffing about maybe a month back and had his nephew run to the alarm tower. Creely's farm was crawling with our townsfolk within maybe fifteen minutes, ready to defend what's ours. One of their more ambitious foot soldiers got a bit overconfident, and ended up with an arrow in his eye up to the fletching. Haven't had any trouble since then."

"I'm glad to hear it, old friend. And thank you for the tip about Moraia. We'll see if we can find her at the market tomorrow. If you don't mind, though," Argus stifled a yawn, "I think I might turn in a bit early. It will be wonderful to sleep in a proper bed."

"I couldn't agree more," Ren smiled. "This place is downright luxurious compared to most of the places I've slept lately. I suspect I'll be snoring in minutes."

Everyone agreed to meet back at the same table the following morning for breakfast, and headed up to their rooms, despite the fact that it was just barely dark out.

As she reached for the door to her quarters, Daijera noticed that the door was open, just a crack. She froze, remembering what *ona* had said about the shifty sand elf. She clicked her tongue, loading venom into the small sacs below her tongue before pushing the door wide open.

Her room was empty, and looked exactly as she had left it, except for one thing. An envelope stood propped against the candlestick on her bed-side table. She closed the door behind her and searched the room thoroughly before reaching for the message.

It was too heavy to contain only paper, and she carefully slid her dagger under the wax seal. She shook the contents–a piece of paper folded around an object–onto the table. She unfolded it gingerly, unsure what chemicals might have been applied to the paper.

The paper had a short message: *I'll be waiting at the dragon an hour after darkness falls.*

The object was an iron coin with a skull on one side.

Chapter 5

Lock and the Skulls

Xexia

Xezia stared at the coin in his palm. It was a sign. It had to be.

Ipthel had said Sora would remain alive, at least as long as there was hope that Xezia would fall in line. It stood to reason then, did it not, that the god would send someone to contact him to try and pass on orders or negotiate a deal? It was the only logical explanation for the coin's mysterious appearance.

He slipped out of the inn stealthily once the sun had set and made his way to the corner where they'd seen the dragon statue. He meant to get there early so he could watch Ipthel's messenger approach. Any edge he could gain might save Sora's life, and his soul.

Please, Epi, he prayed, *help me be clever enough to figure out the right path, and pure enough to resist Ipthel's influence.* He wanted to believe he felt a warm pulse from the amulet against his skin.

The dragon statue was nearly twelve feet of a speckled gray and black stone, and sat upon a base of maybe three additional feet. It occurred to Xezia that there was some irony in the fact that the statue, fairly large by a town's standards, was only a little bit larger than Dalgis if he stood on his hind legs.

The dragon's wings were tucked against its body, and its head dropped low to greet pedestrians with an open-mouthed roar. As fierce as it looked, this creature would have been a juvenile at this size, or so Xezia had read. Dragons were incredibly rare and kept mostly to mountainous regions, so he had never actually seen one.

He was deeply disappointed when he saw Daijera approach several minutes later. She was making no attempt at stealth; rather, she walked toward the statue like a tourist, examining every detail of the beast. After a thorough once-over, she sat on the corner of the large pedestal and pulled out her lute, playing a soft melody that the wind carried to his ears. He noticed that she observed each passerby carefully.

She had received the same coin and message as he had, no doubt, which made him wonder if it was from Ipthel or the Black Moon. He had not reached out to Shar since sending the intel about Aerith, nor had he received any response. Perhaps somehow they'd tracked him here.

Resigning himself to the idea that maybe this wasn't about Sora after all, he stepped out of the doorway where he'd been standing and strode over to Daijera as she picked out a tune.

"About time you made your way over here," she greeted him. "Your lurking was becoming a bit unnerving."

"I thought it wise to watch the area for awhile. I take it you received a coin?"

She nodded. "They're just like the ones we found in Emberell in the tavern." When he shot her a questioning look she added, "I meant to tell you about it, but you didn't seem inclined to talk after...I'm really sorry about Sora. I liked her."

He clenched his jaw and said nothing, but gave a curt nod of acknowledgement.

"Anyway," she continued, "you know those citizens of the town? Well, when Ren and I were investigating the tavern there, they were completely oblivious to our presence. We tried talking to them, but it was like we were invisible. Until I found a box of those coins and touched one. Then they all turned to stare at me. It was...unsettling."

"So the coins aren't some Black Moon signal then," he mused.

"No, I don't think so. But I saw this sand elf in a red cloak hanging around the Silver Branch earlier. I think maybe he left them for us."

"What did he look like?"

"I'm not sure; he kept his hood up, and I could only see about half of his face. Looked like maybe he had a scar on his chin, but it could have been a trick of the light. His arms were fairly thin and his shoulders were stooped, so I couldn't make out his height. He was wearing gloves, which I found odd. The old woman didn't like him much; thinks he's a trouble-maker."

"Why would someone who's trying to be secretive wear a red–"

A brief puff of flame illuminated the dragon's maw, interrupting their conversation. The pair of operatives leapt up to investigate, and found an envelope matching the ones they had found in their quarters propped against the stone teeth.

Xezia snatched it up and, after a quick consultative glance at Daijera, popped open the wax seal and pulled out the paper within.

Just the two of you? How disappointing. You have skills that our organization might find useful, and we have information you might benefit by acquiring, particularly about the substance you have recently encountered. Please bring your coins and use them to buy yourselves a drink at Danalia's Pub, two blocks east. We look forward to formally making your acquaintance.

"A trap?" asked Daijera, giving voice to Xezia's thoughts.

"Almost certainly. But that doesn't mean we shouldn't go. It just means we need to be careful."

"You shouldn't go," came a voice from the other side of the dragon. Xezia pulled his dagger and whipped around, and he heard a soft hiss from Daijera that almost certainly meant she had a weapon of her own at the ready.

"There's no need for that," the voice said. The man in a red cloak stepped out with his gloved hands extended to show that he meant no harm. "I come as a friend. If the Obsidian Skulls want to talk to you, I assure you that *they* aren't looking to make friends."

Daijera made a strange clicking noise, then breathed, "You! You were the elf I saw in the Silver Branch!"

"The very same," he said, bowing slightly at the waist. "Lock Dunach at your service. The choice of whether to keep that appointment is yours to make, of course, but I'd like to offer you a bit of information first so you know what you're up against. Is there somewhere we can speak?"

Xezia and Daijera exchanged looks, and he knew that they were in agreement about the stranger's offer. "We can speak in the stables of the Silver Branch. One of our friends is there, but he can be trusted."

"Ah, yes, the beast. Fascinating, The amount of magic needed to create something like that is staggering. I look forward to meeting him."

Xezia, disarmed by the man's conversational tone, almost smiled in spite of himself. "His name is Dalgis."

"A good name," Lock commented, and as he looked down the street toward their destination, the breeze blew his hood back, revealing a roadmap of scars across two-thirds of his face. His left eye was hidden by a leather patch with a variety of magical symbols embroidered around its edge. The symbol of Epi, a sun rising from behind a cloud, had been branded into the center of the leather.

Xezia felt his heart clench. Had Epi heard his prayer and sent this man to help? He was afraid to entertain the hope, but he couldn't shake the niggling feeling.

After a brief introduction to Dalgis, who was overjoyed to be included in the clandestine conversation, Lock shared his deep reservations about the Obsidian Skulls.

"They're a cult, ultimately," he sighed. "They claim not to be, but that's what they are. They're twisted by their desire for knowledge about Ebon Ichor. They will do anything to learn more about it."

"Ebon Ichor?" Daijera asked, feigning ignorance.

Lock nodded seriously. "It's the black substance you've encountered recently. Less than a week ago, if I'm any judge."

"How can you tell that?" Xezia asked.

"Quite so!" interjected Dalgis. "Are you a seer?"

Lock chuckled drily. "Not at all, I wish I were. I could have avoided so much pain if I'd had better insight." He appeared lost in thought for a moment, then continued. "No, I can tell you've encountered the Ichor because it leaves a...spiritual stench, if you will. The more you are around it, the more those attuned to it can sense it. No doubt that's how they targeted you as well."

"So you've had contact with it then." It was more a statement than a question. Xezia stared at Lock's gloves, understanding creeping into the back of his mind.

"You could say that, yes." After the slightest hesitation, Lock reached up and lifted his eye patch, revealing a blackened and burnt hole where his left eye had once been. "The Skulls can sense that the Ichor has great power, and they seek to control it. They believe they can harness its magic for a variety of purposes, all of them nefarious."

"Can it be controlled?" Xezia asked, feeling the slightest itch in his own blackened finger.

"They think so, but it is my belief that they are being used by larger forces." Lock looked pointedly at Xezia for the briefest of moments.

"Larger?" asked Dalgis. "Like Ironshield?"

"I wouldn't be at all surprised if there were connections to the king and his zealots," Lock agreed.

Daijera took a deep breath. "I think that, since we keep coming across this substance, we should try to learn more about it, and this may be our only opportunity. We've seen some of what it can do, and we have no way to defend ourselves against it."

Xezia nodded but couldn't speak. His mind was filled with thoughts of Sora, clutching a statue of Hoshkn and begging him not to give up.

"I understand the temptation," Lock sighed, "and the choice is yours. But know that nothing they will give you is free. There will be a hefty price."

"Nevertheless," Xezia said, "I think we have to risk it." He looked at Daijera, and she nodded.

"Very well," Lock shook his head. "I will wait here for you. They aren't likely to harm you if you are wise and careful. That said, there is one thing you must not do under any circumstances. You must not mention my name."

Ekko

Ekko sat on the windowsill and sniffed the air with her sensitive vulpine nose. A familiar scent caught her attention; as she looked down to the ground level, she saw Xezia slipping down the alleyway. He was, she suspected, taking an indirect route toward the dragon statue, just as she had planned to do. Apparently the sneak who delivered a coin to her room had made additional stops. She wondered how many. She also wondered why *he* was here. Did he think she wouldn't recognize his scent?

She was about to leap to the next roof to follow Xezia when a sound startled her.

Tuk tuk tuk tuk tuk!

She was so surprised, she almost fell off the ledge. A tiny blue and green head was poking out from the window next door, watching her. She sniffed at Stig, willing him to go away before he attracted Argus's attention.

Uh-owww, uh-oww. He ignored her request and skittered along the wall until he was sitting on the ledge beside her. She growled as softly as she could, warning him to leave her to her business.

TUK TUK! He leapt toward her, and before she could shy away, he had attached his suction-y front feet to her ears, which shouldn't have been possible on fur. *Tuk.* If she wanted to go, he was coming with her, and that's just how it was going to be.

Just a lizard indeed.

Well, if he could stay attached, he could ride along. If he fell off, as she saw it, that wasn't exactly her problem. She made the short leap to the next roof and trotted along the shingles until she reached the edge, then made another jump to the next building, and so on until she got to the corner where she could see the dragon statue. Xezia was hovering in a nearby doorway, waiting to see who showed up for the meeting. After a few minutes, Daijera strolled up to the statue, sat on the base, and began to play a quiet tune on her lute. Xezia walked over to her and they began speaking softly.

Uh-owwww! Stig chirped, and his tone sounded like a warning. There was a rustle of movement in an upstairs window across from Ekko's vantage point. Ekko flattened herself against the roof tiles, and Stig made a soft clucking sound. Ekko felt a tingle of magic run through her frame, and wondered what Stig had just done. She hoped it was a concealment spell. She also made a mental note to have a little chat with Argus later.

A woman's face was just visible in the distant window, and though it was unclear what she was saying, her hand motions indicated that she was casting a spell. Yipping a warning to Xezia and Daijera would do no good; there wasn't time. Fortunately, it didn't appear the mystery woman meant them any harm. A small ball of flame appeared and then instantly extinguished inside the stone dragon's jaws, and once they recovered from being startled, Xezia reached in and pulled out a note.

Ekko looked across the intersection, but the woman in the window was gone, having delivered her message.

The air on the side of the dragon opposite Daijera and Xezia shimmered, and a figure in a red cloak appeared. After a brief exchange, the three of them walked off together back toward the inn. Ekko followed with Stig making little *tuk tuk* noises as they traveled.

Rather than going inside, they went into the stables. Ekko carefully inched along the edge of the thatched roof until she was positioned right above Dalgis's stall. He would catch her scent, no doubt, but she wasn't too worried about him giving her away. She knew she could trust him to conceal her presence.

She had expected a different voice from the one she heard out of the red-cloaked man. This man was clearly a bit older, and certainly had more knowledge than the person she'd been expecting. The information he shared about the Ebon Ichor was deeply disturbing, and she agreed with Daijera when she said they needed to learn what they could.

Daijera and Xezia asked the man for directions, then walked away from the stables together, leaving the man in red chatting with Dalgis.

Tuk tuk tuk! Stig urged her, and she growled softly in response, setting off after the pair as they went to, presumably, keep the meeting the man warned them against.

Ekko dropped to the ground and followed at a distance, keeping to the shadows. When they reached the pub to which they'd been directed, Ekko crept around the perimeter, searching for a window where she could eavesdrop and steal glances of the action.

She saw them get ushered into a back room by a buxom barkeep, so she continued to sneak around back. There didn't seem to be any windows, but like so many of these establishments, the eaves hadn't been maintained properly. She shifted into human form and scrambled up the wooden framework, finding a weak spot in the plaster and thatching, then wedging herself through. It was more than a little annoying that the lizard was still attached to the back of her neck. Then she shifted back and snuggled into a dark corner of the roof thatching so she could watch.

"...that you decided to accept my invitation. I truly believe we can benefit one another with this agreement," a woman's voice was saying. Ekko was pretty sure this was the same woman she'd spotted in the window. The hood of her gray cloak was thrown back, and wild white-blond curls crimped randomly in delicate silver filigree cylinders flowed in all directions. An elaborate black and orange tattoo wound its way up her neck and across a significant portion of her face. In Ekko's experience, that kind of body art was meant to hide scars, maybe even turn them into things of beauty or empowerment. The shapes were abstract, but there seemed to be a motif of flames.

Ekko studied the woman's face. A sun elf, Ekko was almost sure, based on her features, but her skin had a gray undertone. Perhaps some storm elf blood? Her eyes were a shocking green and her lips were full. The smile she wore was clearly forced. Nevertheless, Ekko supposed the woman had once been quite beautiful. Now, though, there was a hardened quality to her, a quality one only earned by surviving some of the worst horrors the world had to offer.

"We haven't agreed to anything just yet," Xezia was saying, "but your elaborate invitation piqued our interest. We thought we should at least hear what you had to say."

The woman nodded emphatically. "Of course! Most wise of you. I must apologize for the rather unorthodox invitation; our organization is misunderstood by many, so we must maintain a certain level of... discretion."

"A sensible precaution," Daijera agreed, surveying the five other individuals in the room, all wearing cloaks similar to the woman's. Each of them had their hands neatly folded on the table in front of them, and each had their hood drawn, so that Ekko couldn't make out their features. "Why don't we put our cards on the table here? You seem to be aware of some of our recent...escapades...though there's no reasonable way you could have that knowledge. Why don't we start there?"

"Oh, dear, I seem to have started this off with an air of distrust. My apologies. Let me back up a little bit, and perhaps that will answer your question as well. My name is Phelia, and I am, as you may have guessed, a user of arcane magicks. I have studied and practiced for much longer than either of you have been alive, I'd wager. I have, you see, a great passion for understanding how the deepest magicks work, and in my travels, I have come across a substance over the last few years that seems to be new to this world."

"You're referring to Ebon Ichor," Xezia volunteered, crossing his arms.

"Yes, marvelous!" Her smile now appeared to be genuine, but there was a hint of predatory glee in it. "It's really shaken up the wizarding academics, as you might imagine. No one seems to know where it came from, or what to do with it."

Xezia's jaw was tight, and Ekko suspected he was thinking about Sora. "It appears to be quite dangerous," he stated noncommittally.

"Have you seen it in action?"

"You could say that, yes. But we don't know much about it. I'm not sure what we could offer you."

Phelia pressed her palms together eagerly. "We...that is, the Obsidian Skulls..." She nodded to her colleagues. "We have managed to contain a quantity of it, and have conducted extensive experiments. We've made some fascinating observations of its behavior."

Ekko noticed the slightest movement along the wall behind Phelia. With her fox eyes, she could just make out the silhouette of a camouflaged lizard. Her ears perked up. She hadn't even been aware that Stig had wandered off. Behind Phelia's seat, stacks of papers were scattered on a low bench. Stig inched toward the papers and...wait...was he eating one of them? Ekko groaned softly. Stupid reptile.

"Behavior? You believe it to be sentient?" Daijera asked.

"After a fashion, yes. And, as you've noted, quite dangerous. It also leaves an...imprint, for lack of a better word...on your aura. That's how we knew you'd come in contact with it."

"So what do you want from us? Sounds like you have more knowledge of it than we do. And yet, here we are, at your *invitation*." Xexia was being deliberately confrontational, probably in an attempt to establish himself as a clever negotiator.

"Ah, yes indeed. Right you are. We'd like to have you as sort of a field team. If you've come across the Ichor once, you're likely to come across it again. We'd like to get a report of your current observations, and we'd also like for you to contact us with any future details which might come to light in the future."

"And in exchange?"

"Right, a fair exchange. If we are able to find a way to protect oneself from its effects, or to fight it, we will share that information with you, naturally."

"Naturally." Daijera and Xezia exchanged glances, and the lamia gave a slight shrug and tilt of her head, a sign that she was deferring to Xezia's decision-making.

"That seems reasonable enough. We know that it can put thoughts in the minds of its victims, make them see things that are painful or frightening."

Phelia's eyes widened and she waved at one of the other figures sitting at the table. The hooded figure began writing down Xezia's account.

"And you were in contact with it when this happened?" Phelia asked.

"Contact, no. Proximity, yes."

"Fascinating!"

"I suppose so," he continued coldly. "We know it can kill people by absorbing them, leaving no trace behind."

Phelia's hand flew to her mouth in horror, and Ekko thought that the woman was laying the act on a little too thick. Surely Xezia saw through it. "That must have been horrible to witness."

Xezia didn't reply. After a brief pause, Daijera stepped in. "That's really about all we learned in our encounter, I'm afraid."

Phelia smiled indulgently. "Still, we've got information we didn't have before. Very useful. I shall give you a messaging scroll so that you can contact me directly with any future information." A hooded woman sitting near the door scampered out of the room, presumably to get the scroll.

Tuk, came a soft sound beside Ekko, and Stig climbed back onto her nape.

"I'll give you one of mine in return," Xezia offered. "That way you can share your research with us as well." He reached into one of his interior cloak pockets and produced two scrolls. He handed them to Phelia, and held her gaze for longer than was typically considered polite before releasing them into her grasp.

A trace of that predatory smile played around her lips again, then disappeared. The door opened and instead of the hooded woman, a young man in a burgundy tunic and leather breeches swaggered into the room with a scroll in one hand, a half-eaten apple (almost certainly stolen) in the other.

Damien, Ekko thought. She fought the temptation to leap off the rafter and claw the ever-present smirk off his face. He tossed the scroll to Phelia and then leaned rakishly against the wall behind her.

"I suppose that concludes our business then." Xezia took the scroll from Phelia and slid it into the pockets of his cloak.

"I look forward to our future exchanges," Phelia said, her eyes boring into his. "I trust they will be...mutually beneficial."

Xezia nodded curtly, and with a slight swish of his robes, he and Daijera exited the room.

"Well, that went better than expected," Phelia said to the group, clearly pleased.

"Sure did," Damien replied, sneaking a glance toward the rafters.

Ekko cursed inwardly and inched out of the crack in the eaves and up onto the roof. She didn't stop running till she got back to the Silver Branch Inn.

Chapter 6

Shades of the Past

Ren

Ren had never felt more clueless than he had at breakfast the next morning.

Colvyn had been kind enough to set up a table and stools in the stable yard so that Dalgis could eat with the rest of the group. Everyone seemed to have had a fairly eventful evening. Everyone, that is, except for Ren.

"Of course I followed you," Ekko was saying. "But I don't trust anonymous notes left on my pillow, thank you very much."

"How ever did you manage to remain unseen?" Argus asked her. He had been looking at her rather pointedly ever since they sat down.

She responded by staring back and hesitating a beat before responding. "I'm a *thief*, Argus. I'm very good at sneaking."

"Mmm hmm," was all he said.

"I can verify that Ekko was, in fact, creeping about and following Xezia and Daijera when they visited me in the stables with that Lock fellow," Dalgis volunteered. "And Argus, my good man, I suspect you are teasing her, since you know she is telling the truth. Stig was with her, after all. I scented them both while I was being introduced."

"Thank you, Dalgis!" Ekko cried in vindication, crossing her arms across her chest. "What about that, Argus? Do you always let your pet roam about in strange cities?"

Argus sniffed derisively and then leaned back, crossing his arms and mirroring her pose. "Stig goes where he wants to," he replied.

"Uhhh-owwww," grumbled Stig, who was contentedly poking at a bowl of grubs.

"Still going to insist that he's just a lizard, Argus?" Xezia asked.

"Now, now, friends," Ren chimed in, growing weary of their sniping, "perhaps the wise thing would be to focus on what we've learned. I'd like to know where you three...uh, four...sorry, Stig...ended up going with this mysterious stranger."

"Not so mysterious, I hope," came a voice from the back door of the inn. Everyone turned as Lock Dunach, slight and somewhat stooped, emerged through the wooden frame and approached the table. "I dare say that that old woman will never trust me, but I assure you that I am completely on the level. You won't get such assurances from Phelia and the Skulls. Or, if you do, they'll be lying. That is where they went, sir. To a meeting of the Obsidian Skulls. I did *not* accompany them."

"Ah, you are the man who met them at the statue, then?" Ren asked.

"I am indeed," he responded, and shook Ren's hand heartily. "No matter what Phelia told you, the Obsidian Skulls are a cult. No doubt she assured you that they were some sort of scientists doing research into a substance which could prove dangerous to this world, but her intentions are much darker than that."

"I thought as much," Daijera said. "Her offer sounded like a sales pitch. She wanted to share information in the name of discovery, but no one with that many scars is an innocent." She hesitated for a split second. "Um, no offense, Lock."

"None taken, good lady," he responded with a touch of irony in his tone. "I came by my scars through darkness and treachery, deeper than you can imagine."

"I can imagine quite a lot," Xezia muttered.

Lock studied him for a moment. "Yes, I imagine you can. I sense the stain of Corruption on your life, far stronger than on your friends here. The stench of Ipthel has been on you since childhood, I'd wager."

"His zealots destroyed my village when I was eight," Xezia replied simply, as though this event was of no more import than the changing of the seasons. "More recently, he took my friend. I aim to see her returned."

A cloud passed over Lock's eyes for a brief moment and then was gone. "My son, we should talk more of these things. I regret to say that I am familiar with Ipthel's ways; perhaps I can be of some service to you in your quest."

"Speaking of that," Ekko stood up from her seat and began balancing her dagger on her thumb, like a circus performer practicing an act, "why exactly did you feel compelled to approach us? Do you go around searching for people who have encountered this goop, or do you just stalk people the Obsidian Skulls show interest in?"

"A good question, young lady...Ekko, is it? I'm afraid you may think me a bit mad when you hear my answer, and to be honest, you may be right. I had a dream vision several days ago. There was lightning in the sky, and voices...so many voices! Then the storm clouds parted, and a little girl was there, singing to herself and dancing. In each hand, she held a wand of ribbons...the kind that fae dancers use, you know? A stick with ribbons attached to one end? Anyhow, each of her sticks had three ribbons, and when I approached her, she stopped dancing and handed the sticks to me. *They're coming,* she told me. *The Six are coming.*" Lock looked around at the faces of the party. "I saw your party arrive at the Silver Branch, and I sensed the stain of an encounter with Corruption on you. When I realized you numbered six, I felt it was a sign. I believe She meant you. That you were coming, and I was meant to assist you however I could."

"She? Who is *she*? Some child in a dream?" Xezia asked, his voice laced with bitterness.

"She's Epi, of course."

Xezia's snarky expression went blank and he fell silent.

Lock continued, "I told you I had knowledge of Ipthel's ways, and I shall tell you more about that in time. What you must know is this: I was lost–oh, so lost–for so long, but at my lowest moment, I felt the touch of Epi upon me. Only Purity herself could have pulled my poor soul from its depths, and I have sought to serve Her ever since. I believe, with all that I am, that She led me to you. I know not what you seek, but I am here to help you in Her service." He bowed deeply.

"Are you a mage?" Ren inquired. "Have you taken a vow to Epi's service?" Something was nagging at him, as though they were only seeing half the picture.

"Alas, no, I am merely a wizard. No temple would have me as a sworn mage. But I do have a goodly amount of knowledge and magical skill, all of which is at your disposal."

"I don't know," Ekko said, pulling out another dagger and proceeding to juggle them, the morning sunlight flashing off of the blades in reflection, "I feel like there is more here than meets the eye..." She whipped around suddenly and flung one of the daggers into a haypile against the stableyard wall. The other clattered harmlessly onto the dirt.

"OW!" came a voice from within, and a young man of perhaps nineteen years stumbled out of the pile with Ekko's dagger buried in his left arm. "Dammit, Ekko! What was that for?"

"You know very well what that was for, Damien, you lousy rat! You let me get arrested for what YOU did!"

"Well, you broke out, didn't you? I knew you would. No holding cell could contain you for long." Damien pulled out the dagger and a red stain began spreading across his shirt sleeve. "I really liked this shirt, too," he complained.

"I hope the wound gets infected, and you get gangrene, and die a horribly, smelly death," Ekko pouted.

Damien tossed the dagger aside and started walking toward her, but Dalgis stepped in front of him.

"I may look friendly, young man," Dalgis warned through his pointed teeth, his voice low, "but I assure you that I have eaten things much larger than you. I would think very carefully about how you intend to proceed."

Damien froze in his tracks and fear flashed across his face for an instant. Then the smirk returned and he regarded Dalgis steadily, "I see Ekko has significantly improved the quality of people she hangs around with."

Dalgis drew himself up to his full height, looming over the boy, then snuck a side glance at Ekko.

"It's okay, Dalgis. If he gets out of line, you can shred him. Damien, why are you here? And why are you working for the Skulls?"

"Ah, now THOSE are the right questions to ask." He ripped off his sleeve and used the cloth to bind his wound. "But you asked in the wrong order. I am working with the Skulls because I owe them a marker. Phelia and her nutty friends there got me out of a little jam awhile back, so I've been running errands for them ever since. But I don't like her, and if you want my personal opinion, the whole lot of them are bonkers. Which brings me to your other question. I'm here to change teams. Once I realized you were in town, I figured it was a good chance to cut my losses and move on to a better situation, you know?"

"What the hell makes you think I'd let you come anywhere with me? After what you did? You're the one who killed that guy, and you let me take the fall for you! They were going to *hang* me!"

"Oh, you know very well they'd never get that far. Your...unique skills...pretty much guaranteed your escape. I would never have been able to get away. I don't...have those skills. And I couldn't be sure you'd be able to break me out before they stretched my neck."

"Your friend here sounds like quite a despicable fellow," Dalgis commented to Ekko. "Are you certain I shouldn't dispatch him?"

Ekko patted Dalgis's flank. "No. Not yet anyway." She turned back to Damien. "But I also can't think of a single reason why we should take you with us."

"How about because I know where your family is?"

Ekko spat on the ground. "Who cares?"

"Okay, how about because I know a bit about Phelia's plans for that black stuff?"

"That might actually be useful," Ren piped in.

"Kaack kaack kaaaack," Stig began hacking over his bowl.

"I am very good at being useful," Damien offered, a sly smile crossing his face as though he knew he'd won.

"Kaaaaaaack!"

"Good heaven, Argus, is Stig alright?" Ren asked as the lizard's tongue protruded a little more with each convulsion. "Is he choking on something?"

Argus reached over and rubbed Stig's sides vigorously. "What have you got there, Stig?"

"Kaaaack!" From out of Stig's mouth popped a slimy wad of paper.

"What in the world?" Daijera asked.

"It's a map," reported Argus, spreading the paper flat while Stig, looking very pleased with himself, resumed eating a particularly fat grub.

"A map of what?" Ren looked over Argus's shoulder, and a chill ran through him as he recognized the geographical features of the Rosend/Ironshield border.

"A map to one of the Skulls' research facilities," Damien answered, grabbing a piece of bread and a hunk of cheese off the table, "and I can get you in undetected."

Lock

The walk to the market was not a particularly long one, and Lock hung to the back of the group so he could speak to the young man with the blackened aura.

"Your name is Xezia, is it not?"

The man's head had been hanging, a sense of hopelessness clouding his features. He nodded, barely looking up.

"Ipthel has been hard on you, boy. I can smell him polluting you even now." He meant for the comment to be empathetic.

"Thanks so much," Xezia replied drily. "Always nice to know that the funk of Corruption itself has become my natural odor."

Lock smiled, his scars stretching with the effort, despite the surly reply. "It is a spiritual stench, but unmistakable to another who wore it for so long. Do you serve Him willingly?" He held his breath, hoping for a negative answer.

"What does it matter? The result is the same."

"Son, what hold does He have over you? If you do not serve Him by choice, then why not break His hold on you? Serve another?"

"I tried that, old man." Xezia tilted up his chin and opened his shirt to reveal a blackened symbol of Epi hanging from a leather strap. "All it got me was false hope. The bastard has been toying with me for years."

Lock recognized the bitterness in Xezia's voice. His own had sounded very similar not so many years ago. "Was it false hope? Truly? You still wear Purity's symbol. That speaks to at least some spark within you which craves redemption."

"What I want means nothing if I am not wanted in return," Xezia replied, and the sadness and ache within him echoed through his words.

"You are wanted, son. I assure you. If Epi can redeem a lost soul like mine, surely She can help you as well." The Ichor in Xezia's blood called out to the old wizard, the promise of power thick in the air.

"I don't doubt that She can," he snipped, "but then why hasn't She done so? Surely She could have stepped in at any time. I have prayed and prayed to Her, put all my faith in Her. And yet, here I am, in Corruption's snare."

"Opposing deities can't interfere with each other directly in the way you are implying, Xezia. Their energies cancel out. We are the scales that keep the balance. People, I mean. If Ipthel had his claws in you early in life, Epi could not simply slap his hand away, even if you asked. But there is a way. It would not be easy, and it would likely be painful in more ways than one. But the path to Epi is still open to you. As I said, She brought me back to myself, and I was far more gone than you are now."

Xezia looked at him askance, but there was a glimmer in his eye, and Lock's heart beat faster. Then the look faded, and his shoulders drooped again.

"There's more to it than just my soul. I would endure any pain to free myself, but I would also endure any pain to free Sora from his grasp." His voice broke as he mentioned the name.

"Is she your...wife?" Lock asked carefully, suspecting one of the tricks Ipthel worked so well.

"No, a dear friend, but if I can get her back, if I can save her, then maybe..." Choked with emotion, Xezia could not finish.

Lock's heart broke for him. Ipthel's playbook was expansive, but oh, how the evil god enjoyed holding the life of a loved one over a prospective follower's head.

"Oh, my boy, surely you must know that Ipthel will not honor any promise he makes you."

"I'm aware of that," Xezia's expression hardened, "but if there's any chance to rescue her, I must try. I must...fight. For her."

Lock laid his hand on the man's arm. "I understand. Truly I do. But in all the years I was under his thumb...and that was many decades...he never returned a soul he had taken. Not for any reason."

"I can't let myself believe that," Xezia muttered, and his voice sounded much younger than his years. "I can't give up on her."

Lock nodded, knowing that if this Sora was alive, she was far worse off than if she had died. And Ipthel was probably saving her as leverage. That was His way. "I shall pray to Epi. Perhaps she can find a way through for you."

Xezia fell into troubled silence as they approached the market, and Lock's soul felt burdened. This young man (part elf, certainly, but the other features could belie a half-dozen other races) was much like he had been. If someone had acted to save him so many years ago, how many lives could have been spared?

I will find a way, he thought. *I will bring your soul back from the brink and deny Ipthel his prize. Even if I have to give my own miserable life to do it.*

Chapter 7

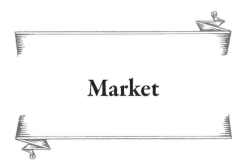

Market

Elia

If someone had told her a year ago that she'd be traipsing all over Rosend, a fugitive and an adventurer, Elia would have told them they'd been eating the wrong mushrooms. If someone had told her that she'd have brushes with the Deities themselves, even at the fringes of Their awareness, she would have told them they were descending into madness.

And yet here she was.

A fugitive.

An adventurer.

On the fringes of godly awareness.

And she wasn't really sure how she felt about it. Life had been simple in Breadstone. She had lived with Aunt Mita until her passing, and then she had kept the cottage and taken employment in an herbalist's shop so she'd have enough money to eat and pay her taxes. Maybe a little extra to eat at Argus's tavern now and then if she didn't feel like cooking.

Eventually she probably would have married; certainly a couple of young men had come around courting her. They had been nice enough, Dorin and Rove, but they weren't curious about things, and they couldn't hold an interesting conversation. So she'd managed to discourage them both before either of them got serious enough about her to start thinking about permanence.

"What's on your mind?" She was startled out of her reverie by Ren's voice.

"I was thinking about how much my life has changed in these past few months," she answered honestly.

"For the better or the worse?"

She smiled ruefully. "Depends on the day. When I was conscripted into Godfroy's army, I thought that was a travesty, and my only plan was to survive long enough to go home and back to my quiet life. But now? I'm not so sure."

"My dear girl, are you implying that you'd prefer a life of uncertainty and danger to the safety of your home village?" He seemed amused.

"I'm not sure," she shrugged. "I used to think I truly loved my life in Breadstone. I loved Aunt Mita, certainly, but when she died..." her voice trailed off for a moment as she pictured the face of the kind woman who had raised her. "I guess I loved my job working with the town herbalist, but I think it was mostly because I was always learning new things. Other than that, Breadstone was, well, sort of boring."

"And you prefer the adventure?" He seemed surprised, and maybe a little amused.

"That's what I'm trying to figure out. I don't particularly like my life always being in peril, but I like the challenge of it all. Each day is something new. And it seems like what we're doing actually matters."

"It must, if the Deities are inserting themselves."

"Exactly! It's like what we're doing might actually help lots and lots of people. Maybe even end the war! Maybe even get rid of Godfroy!"

Ren spit on the ground at the mention of the Blood King. "Nothing would please me more," he said, a trace of bitterness in his voice.

"It's like...and please, Ren, don't laugh at me...it's like ever since Emberell, since Imogen...this all fits. Like I'm supposed to be here. I've never felt like that before."

Ren smiled. "I believe we are all exactly where we are meant to be."

Elia shook her head, feeling like maybe he was missing the weight of what she was saying. Maybe no one else could really understand. But she knew she was meant to do more...*be more*...than an herbalist's assistant.

The main square of Verwoerd was bustling as they passed through the gates of the inner city. Carts and tables ringed a large stone building with a statue of the familiar dual image of Utrui in front of its entrance. Elia surmised that this must be the seat of government offices for the town, and commerce was thriving all around it.

Throngs of people bustled from stand to stand, carrying baskets overflowing with their purchases for the week. Merchants called out to shoppers, hoping to tempt them with the softest or cheapest fabrics, the brightest apples, the sweetest jams and jellies. Elia could see Colvyn ahead, chatting with Argus as they walked. Xezia and Lock were in deep conversation, and Ekko was riding on Dalgis's back. Daijera seemed to be enjoying browsing the carts, until she spotted a fortune-teller's tent and seemed suddenly disturbed. They passed by merchant after merchant, and then she saw the elf point to a corner booth up ahead.

Booth was hardly the right word. It was an explosion of colors and textures. The cover had been removed from a transport wagon, and racks of potted plants covered every inch of the frame. Green ribbons rippled in the wind, and the scents of dozens of flowers floated throughout the market. A crowd of people pressed around the proprietor, and Elia gasped when she saw her: a tall fae woman with skin and hair the color of terracotta clay, and eyes like a cloudless summer sky. She radiated friendliness despite the clamor, talking to each customer in laughing alto tones.

Colvyn called for the group to wait while he made his way to the front to speak to Moraia. He leaned forward and spoke to her softly, and as he spoke, the woman searched the crowd until her eyes found them. Elia wouldn't have thought it possible for Moraia to appear more beautiful, but the smile that spread across her face as she scanned the party was like watching the rising of the summer sun. Moraia was, as far as Elia could tell, the personification of the beauty of nature. The lovely fae muttered something back to Colvyn and he nodded, then returned to where the group was standing.

"Moraia says she's happy you made it, whatever that means," Colvyn chuckled. "She also says it's too chaotic to have so important a conversation right now, but she will come to the Silver Branch this afternoon after the market closes. That gives us about four hours. But she seems very excited to speak with you. Looks like *ora-ini*'s suggestion was a good one."

"Does that mean we have a little time for shopping?" Daijera asked.

"I'd say so. Do you think you can find your way back to the inn by yourself?" Daijera laughed in response and disappeared into the crowd of customers. Argus, Lock, Xezia and Colvyn decided to return to the inn, and Ekko and Dalgis decided they'd like to see some of the farms on the edge of town.

"Well, my dear, would you like to accompany an old-ish fellow like me on a stroll through the market?" Ren offered his arm as official escort.

"I'd be delighted," Elia smiled back at him and looped her arm through his, hoping to find some rare sweets she might buy to keep her spirits up on the long journey that lay ahead.

Elia was in her room nibbling on the sugared dates she had bought when there was a quiet tap on her door. She opened it to find Ekko, flushed with sun from her time out with Dalgis, and wearing a crown of daisies on her head. "Moraia's here," she reported. "Come on down to the stableyard. Hey, are those sugared dates?" Before Elia could reply, Ekko swiped a date and popped it in her mouth, then turned and bounded down the stairs. Elia sighed heavily and followed.

The scene in the stableyard was downright comical. Everyone was gathered around the table, smiling and bedecked in wreaths of flowers. Everyone, that is, except for Argus, who was, in fact, wearing flowers in his hair, but looked rather like he'd just swallowed sour milk.

"OH! THERE SHE IS!" Moraia leapt up from her seat and dashed forward, scooping Elia up in a bone-crushing hug. "I'm just overjoyed to meet you!" she effused, releasing Elia and hanging a necklace of tiny pink roses around her neck. "These are just perfect for you! You are just the most lovely little thing!" She held Elia's cheeks in her hands for a moment and sighed joyfully, then glided back to her seat at the table. Elia stood still for a moment, overwhelmed with awkwardness, then sat down as well.

"Look, Elia," Dalgis beamed. "Moraia brought me flowers that match my feathers!" He grinned as only Dalgis could, and fluffed up his frill against a wreath of nasturtiums. "And are you prepared for the best part? They're *edible*. So when they start to wilt, I can have them as a snack! Is that not the most thoughtful gift?"

"Uh, yes indeed, Dalgis," Elia stammered. "Thank you for the flowers, Moraia."

"Oh, absolutely my honor and pleasure. I'm so happy you are all here! I've been hearing of your coming in the rustles of leaves for weeks, and I've been ever so excited!"

"Does that mean you can help us find the Book of Hohn?" Ekko asked.

"Ah, straight to the point, Ekko my dear. I can help, after a fashion. That is, I can help point you in the right direction. I do not guard the Book, but you have Hohn's blessing upon you, so you may yet reach the place you need to go. Indeed, the fact that you have made it this far means that She has dropped clues for you here and there."

"We did get one clue from Fufei, a high priestess of Hohn, who told us..."

"Oh! Fufei? I *ADORE* Fufei."

"Uh, yes. Just so. Anyhow, she told us to follow the lightning, so we thought perhaps we should head toward the domain of the storm elves." Argus picked a daisy out of his sideburns.

Moraia clapped her hands like a proud parent. "Yes, yes indeed! You must go to their capital city!"

"They have a capital city?" Elia asked. She wasn't sure why, but she'd always assumed storm elves lived in caves or something.

"But of *course* they do," Moraia giggled, a tinkly sound like wind chimes. "They have a very complex and fascinating culture."

"No doubt from their isolation," Daijera mumbled, clearly in a foul mood despite the black-eyed susans woven into her hair.

"Oh, yes indeed. That is most certainly why," Moraia continued, undeterred. "You must go to their capital and wait for a sign. There will most certainly be a sign. Something familiar in a place that is not."

"There's a small problem, though," Argus pushed. "We don't know where it is, and none of us speak the language."

"Oh, pish posh. Language is artificial. You can certainly manage. It's not as though you're negotiating a treaty. And you need not worry. Hohn will make sure you find your way."

"So we're supposed to rely on faith and hope to get us there?" Xezia asked acidly.

"Well, naturally," she laughed. "It's gotten you this far."

Daijera

She was pretty sure Xezia hadn't even noticed the tent, because he was so deep in conversation with Lock Dunach that he wasn't really paying attention as they walked through the marketplace. The fact that he *hadn't* noticed was adding to her concern. Without Sora to anchor him, the mage was becoming increasingly unstable, and though she was sworn to watch his back, she wasn't so sure he'd return the favor, Loyalty Code or no.

At the first opportunity to break away from the group, Daijera bolted into the crowd and, in a very roundabout and wandering way, made her way back to the fortune teller.

To an ordinary patron of the market, this would look like any common tent for people to have their palms, or tea leaves, or auras read. Every market of this size had at least one purported seer selling his or her wares. More often than not, that person was a charlatan. In this case, however, the owner of the tent was a gatekeeper to Black Moon.

The tent itself was not terribly large, perhaps the size of two large dining tables laid side by side. Its deep purple curtained sides flapped gently in the breeze, but still obscuring what went on within, and the golden stars embroidered into the fabric glinted in the morning sun. It was a common four-sided tent design, with a square frame and a center pole creating a peaked roof. It was on that peak that she'd spotted it. The ornament at the top was a globe of black obsidian. A Black Moon.

It was possible that she was wrong of course, but she doubted it. She would pay for having her fortune told, then drop a few cryptic statements that a Black Moon operative would recognize, and go from there.

A pair of young elven maidens stumbled out of the tent as Daijera approached. They were giggling and clinging to each other, and she surmised that they were likely sisters.

"Did you hear what she told me? Within the year, I'll be engaged to a handsome and charming merchant! Within the year!"

"You're so lucky," the other whined. "She couldn't see my future at all!"

"Oh, don't be sad! Perhaps your future isn't set..."

The girls blended into the crowd, drunk on the excitement of a perceived glimpse into the future. Daijera rolled her eyes. The fortune teller was almost certainly a grifter. Seeing no one approaching, she slipped into the tent, her eyes shocked by the dimness within. She felt the tingle of protective wards as she passed through them.

"Come in, come in!" said a crackly voice. "Let us see what the future holds for you, my lovely one."

Daijera's eyes adjusted to the darkness quickly, and she found herself looking down at a gnomish woman of indeterminate, but clearly advanced, age. It was an impressive glamour, but for one who wore an illusory face daily, the vibration of the spell was unmistakable.

"I pay my respects, ancient one," Daijera began smoothly. "I seek your wisdom and counsel." She pulled two silvers out of her wrist purse and laid them on the table, which was cluttered with books, a scrying bowl filled with water, a silken bag which almost certainly contained runes, and a collection of feathers circling a burning candle.

"You are a wise one yourself," said the gnome. "I am Aarna, and I am at your service, my dear. What is it you seek?"

"I am at a crossroads in my life," Daijera replied, "pulled this way and that, just as the moon pulls the tide." She made sure to make direct eye contact as she mentioned the moon, hoping to draw a reaction.

Aarna's eyes narrowed. "So you seek guidance? Or a peek at what the future holds for you?"

"Guidance, certainly. And connection. I am hoping you can point my steps on a path where I might find others like myself."

"Indeed?" The gnome took Daijera's hand in hers and began examining her palm closely. "It appears you are torn, my dear, between old friends and new friends. Do I hit it right?"

"You would not be wrong to say so. But it is not so much by choice. My travels have taken me far from home, and I am out of place here. I am, I think, missing my old friends somewhat. I want to go home." The admission surprised her, but she realized that it was true. This assignment was far more than she had bargained for, and fairly significantly outside her normal skillset.

"What stops you from doing so?"

Daijera hesitated, not sure if her doublespeak was being understood, and if the gnome was testing her in return. "I have accepted employment with a traveling company, and the tour has gone on much longer than was originally agreed upon."

"So why do you need my guidance, young one?"

"When I accepted this job, I made an Oath of Loyalty, and despite the fact that I feel I am not where I should be, I would not make myself an oathbreaker."

"That is wise, child. There are consequences in the Universe for such things."

"I seek your wise counsel, hoping that perhaps the stars and moon above might be able to tell me if I've fulfilled my contract and would be welcomed back home."

"That is an odd question to ask the spirits."

"Is it?"

"Indeed it is. May I touch your head, child? Perhaps the shape of your skull will yield some wisdom." The gnome climbed up on the table and reached out with both hands.

Despite a strong aversion to letting anyone touch her head, Daijera felt strongly that this was a test of obedience. She bowed her head into the gnome's hands. Tiny fingers probed her scalp, and Aarna made the occasional *hmmm* sound, as though she were considering the implications of this bone shape or that curve of the skull. But when Aarna gently pushed Daijera's ear forward, revealing the small tattoo on the back of her earlobe marking her as a Black Moon operative, the older woman laughed and removed her hands.

"I believe we can end this ridiculous charade now, sister," Aarna said, plopping back into her chair.

Daijera raised her eyes, and instead of the wizened old woman she'd seen before, a middle-aged goblin with a shock of black hair and curved, pointed teeth sat across from her. She pulled up her earlobe to expose her own tattoo, assuring Daijera that she was safe.

"A goblin, huh? I don't see too many of your lot these days," Daijera chuckled.

"No more unusual than a lamia headed north, wouldn't you agree?"

"You've got me there."

"So what is this about? Clearly you aren't part of our local contingency," Aarna began swirling her finger in the bowl of water.

"You're right about that. I'm on assignment. But I think this particular job has moved outside my area of expertise. I'd like to get in touch with someone in leadership to see if they'd like to replace me with a different operative."

"That's a fairly bold request, don't you think?"

"Perhaps, but can it be done?"

"Possibly. But no one here would be privy to your assignment, I'm guessing."

Daijera hadn't really considered the logistics of her request. "No, I suppose not." She thought for a minute, then had an idea. "Would you be able to facilitate contact with a distant chapter officer?"

"For a price, I might. How distant?"

"Swanford. I'd like to contact Shar of the Swanford chapter. I have a scroll, but I think that method would be ineffective in this case."

"Yes, I do see what you mean. You're looking for a quick conversation. And I'm looking for payment."

"What would your price be?" Daijera asked, well aware that goblins tended to be unscrupulous where money was concerned.

"How much have you got?"

Daijera laughed. "Nice try, but this isn't my first day on the job. What's your price? I'll pay it if I can."

Aarna sniffed, somewhat disappointed. "I'm more interested in relics than money. Do you have anything of magical value? Something that might bring good resale?"

Daijera considered the items she had in her bag. None of them were magical in nature except for the scroll Shar had given her. And that was far too common to be of value. She slid her hand into her shoulder bag and felt the items within, keeping her eye on Aarna while she searched. When her fingers brushed against something smooth and cool, she had an idea.

"Well, I don't know if this will hold much value to you, but I did pilfer it from a wizard's workshop." She pulled one of Zaos's crystals out and set it on the table. "Smoky quartz, I believe. Wand cut, and good quality. I'm not sure if it's actually magical, but I imagine it would fetch a good price amongst wizards."

The goblin's eyes sparkled, and she began to reach for the crystal.

"Uh-uh," Daijera said, closing her hand over the stone. "Do we have a deal?"

"We do, but on one condition. I get the stone even if you don't get the answer you want."

"Deal."

"I need something this Shar person has touched. You said you have a messaging scroll?"

Daijera produced it from her bag and handed it to the goblin, who spread the parchment out on the table, anchoring the corners with items from the table. Aarna began muttering in the guttural goblin language, dipping her finger into an inkpot and tracing sigils on the parchment with her pointed fingernail. The only word Daijera could make out was Shar's name. Aarna finished drawing her sigils and looked up.

"You only have as long as the smoke lasts, maybe two or three minutes. Get to the point quickly." Then she ran her inked fingernail through the flame of the candle, and the first sigil began to dissipate in a thin stream of smoke. As the stream curled and twisted, Shar's face appeared, looking surprised.

"DAIJERA? IS THAT YOU? What in the world...?"

"No time for pleasantries, I'm afraid," Daijera interrupted, and Aarna nodded. "We've continued north, and, well, this is a much more complex operation than we originally thought. Looks like we might end up stepping on Ironshield's toes, and..."

"You're in Ironshield?"

"No, no, I'm still in Rosend, but pretty close to the border. Anyway, you know how the king was interested in the same prize we're after?

Well, it appears he has other...projects... going on as well. I think you need warriors up here, not me." The first sigil was gone and the second began to turn to smoke.

"I thought Sora was the muscle out of you three?"

"Sora...Sora's dead. Probably. Most likely. At any rate, she's gone."

"How did that happen?"

"I'll tell you all about it someday, but I can't take the time right now. I feel like I'm a bit out of my depth here, and without Sora, well, Xezia seems a bit unpredictable. I don't think he'll endanger the mission, but you really need someone up here that would be better in combat."

Shar thought for a moment, and by the time she spoke again, the second sigil had burned out. Only one remained.

"Listen, Daijera, as much as I'd like to call you back to Swanford so we could drink and sing songs of the sea, I think Allistair would want you to stay with this and keep gathering intelligence. Hire mercenaries if you have to, but I think you're going to have to stay the course for now."

"Are...are you sure? I will always do my best, of course, but..."

"Have you found it yet?"

Something in her tone set Daijera's internal alarm bells ringing. There was an uncharacteristic urgency, perhaps even underlying desperation. "We have a lead and are heading to the northern Rosend-Ironshield border."

Shar nodded. "Keep in touch. Allistair wants to get his hands on...it...before anyone else does."

Disappointment flooded through Daijera's veins. This mission was too messy, too complicated, and too long. "Okay, Shar, but..." and before she could finish her sentence, the last sigil burned away and Shar was gone.

"Well, dearie, sorry you didn't get your way, but a deal's a deal." Aarna's appearance shimmered, and the glamour of the elderly gnome returned, her palm extended.

"Of course. A deal's a deal." Daijera handed over the crystal and stood.

"Good luck, my lovely. Sounds like you've got a hard road ahead of you," Aarna smiled, and her tone actually sounded sincere.

"You have no idea." Daijera nodded and slipped back out into the sunlight, her heart full of darkness.

Chapter 8

A Hell of a Bargain

Xezia

He lay awake that night, thinking of Lock Dunach and the warnings he was trying to impart. It meant something to Xezia that Lock was so determined to save his soul...not for his own gain, but to save Xezia from suffering as he had.

But there was one hole in Lock's entire approach: he was writing off Sora as lost. It's not that he was wrong; he was probably right, but Xezia couldn't afford to think that way. No, Ipthel wouldn't have destroyed Sora if He still wanted something. He'd need to dangle her like a carrot for a stubborn mule in order to keep Xezia in line. There was no doubt in Xezia's mind that she was safe somewhere. Maybe not comfortable, but certainly alive.

As he let his eyes soak in the darkness of the room, he was startled by the sound of a fire igniting. There was a small glow hovering just outside his window. It appeared to be a small sphere of flames, roughly the size of a nondi melon. He leapt up to look outside, and the ball bounced merrily outside the glass, as if it were waiting.

Curiosity got the best of him, as it always did. After verifying that his nighttime pitcher was full of water, he opened the window, and the ball spun before him as if showing off a new trick.

"Hello there, Xezia," Phelia's voice crackled from within the fire. "Somehow, I felt as if you and I weren't quite done with our conversation."

"What makes you think that?" His eyes scanned the alley and surrounding streets, at least as far as he could see. At the far end of the alley, the strange woman stepped out of the shadows for a moment and waved. "That's a neat trick," he commented.

"Oh, I have quite a lot of neat tricks," she said, and even without being able to see her face, he could tell that she had a wicked smile on her lips. She wasn't playing the benign researcher now. "I suspect it won't be long before you have some tricks of your own."

"What do you mean by that?"

"Oh, surely you know that you've been hand-picked for some great destiny?" She was baiting him, but she also seemed to know far more than she should.

"So I've been told," was his wry response.

"You don't sound excited to be the Dark God's little golden boy."

"I'm no one's golden boy. What do you want, Phelia?"

She chuckled and the flames flickered. "Well, I'd be lying if I didn't admit to being a bit jealous. I've been working very hard for His favor for years. I'm not ungrateful, mind you; He's gifted me with enormous power. But you? You're his CHOSEN. Doesn't seem fair, does it?"

"I suppose not. Feel free to take my ranking position. I don't want it."

"What is it that you DO want?" The question was unexpected.

"What do you mean by that?" he asked, wary of sharing more than she already knew.

"I mean that you are no true believer. Our Lord is forcing your service somehow. Did He offer you a bargain? Or perhaps a temptation you couldn't refuse?"

"You're out of your mind if you think I'm going to lay my soul bare for you. You've basically told me that you're an enemy. That's a terrible persuasion tactic, by the way."

"Oh, tut tut, Xezia. I'll admit I have no fondness for you, but I think we could help each other. We both want something, and we can help each other get it."

"Nice try. Why would I trust you?"

"Oh, you definitely shouldn't trust me. But I am a girl who loves bargains. You want something that He has. I want the power that He means to grant you, because it should be mine anyway. And I think we can both achieve our goals by taking the same path."

"What in the Skies are you talking about?" Xezia snorted, but he couldn't deny being intrigued.

"There is a certain...artifact...which could grant both of our wishes, you see. Even if what we want runs counter to what He wants."

"You're talking about His Book..." Xezia's eyes grew wide in surprise. Why would she approach him, a total stranger, with so bold a plan? It seemed like a trap. And yet...there was an undeniable logic to what she said. The Book of Corruption might be the one thing that would allow him to circumvent Ipthel's games.

"Oh, there you go. Good puppy. Yes, the Book. I can't go looking for it, but you have the lingering vibration in your aura of one of the Books, unless I miss my guess. Nothing else could leave so strong an imprint. Other than the touch of a Deity, of course, which you also pulse with. That would be His, I expect."

"What does Corruption's book contain?" he asked, playing along, trying to determine how far her inside knowledge extended.

"I've never seen the real one, of course, but if the lore of the six Books speaks true, then each book contains spells and other arcane knowledge meant only for each Deity's Champion. The true question, of course, is whether one must BE the chosen Champion to use the book, or whether possessing the Book can make one INTO a Champion."

"I have read something vague about Champions, but what are they? Some sort of earthly representative of each deity?"

"Much much more, puppy. They are imbued with some sliver of the deity's power, and they are granted immortality. A pretty sweet arrangement, wouldn't you say?"

"So what makes you think I'd give that up, if that's what Ipthel has in mind for me?"

"Because you ooze grief, Xezia. Something–or more likely *someone*–has been taken from you. And without that something or someone, you have no interest in immortality."

"You seem to think you know me pretty well."

"Maybe not you, but I know your type. You crave power, not for its own sake, but so that no one can hold it over you."

"But that's not you, I suppose? Why would I ever enter into a deal with you?"

"Because I offer you a blood oath. I will feed you information and help you find what you seek. And when you find the Book, you get what you want from it, and then turn it over to me. Once I have it, Ipthel will make me his new Champion, and you can go away and do whatever it is you want to do. With your life intact and my favor."

Xezia considered this. Phelia would definitely betray him without a second thought, but a blood oath was binding. And it seemed that what she offered was mutually beneficial.

"I'll think about it," he said carefully.

She chuckled again, and the fiery ball began to spin and shrink. "What is it that you want, Xezia? Tell me."

"Sora," he whispered. "I want Sora's life and safety."

And with a soft *whoosh*, the flames were gone and he was alone in the dark.

Dalgis

"Those are the terms, Damien. You talk to me with Dalgis present, or you don't talk to me."

"He said he would eat me, Ekko."

"To be completely fair," Dalgis interjected, "she stabbed you first. So you are in no more or less danger with me present. Well, probably a little bit more, but that's really your own fault."

Damien regarded Dalgis with what appeared to be annoyance, but based on his heart rate, it was more likely fear.

"Fine," the boy said. "If that's the only way." He turned to Ekko and did his best to pretend that Dalgis wasn't taking up two-thirds of the stall. A horse three stalls down whinnied and snorted as if in sympathy. "I want to get away from these Obsidian Skulls, Ekko. They're maniacs."

"Then why are you working with them? It's not like you have a problem reneging on a deal. So they saved your life. Great. That's their own stupid fault. Just leave."

"You don't understand. That woman, Phelia, she..." and here he shuddered, "...she knows things. And she can do things. Unnatural things. If I ran, she'd find me and kill me."

"Would she not do the same if you were escaping with us?" Dalgis offered.

"Not if she thought I was still working for her."

"What do you propose, young man?"

"You take me with you and I'll promise her that I'll spy on you and give her regular updates. You'd be able to approve every single update, of course. But I somehow never made it back, well, maybe she'd just forget about little old me."

"So let me get this straight," Ekko hopped up on a hay bale and crossed her legs. "You want us to *agree* to let you spy on us for someone you acknowledge is a maniac. You've completely lost your mind, Damien."

Damien ran his fingers through his black hair in exasperation. "I know how it sounds, but I can give you information. Valuable information."

"Oh, I do like information," came a voice from the far end of the stable. Daijera sauntered into the stable, seemingly unconcerned about whether or not her presence was desired. Her eyes were flat and calculating, and she was in as foul a mood as Dalgis had ever seen her. "I also happen to be very good at striking bargains with spies." She bit her lip, as though she hadn't meant to disclose that last part, but recovered seconds later. "With your permission, of course, Ekko, I think I can be helpful here, as I have no emotional stake in this *boy*." She emphasized the last word as she stared at him.

"Oh, well, I..." Ekko hesitated, perhaps unsure of Daijera's motives.

"If you are experienced in negotiation," Dalgis replied, "then perhaps a somewhat neutral party would be beneficial." He also wasn't sure of her motives, but he was quite sure that the only one who should be worried was Damien.

"Alright, Dalgis, if you think so."

Daijera smiled, a predatory flash in her eyes, and turned to Damien. "We need to start with you giving us more information. How, precisely, did you end up working with these people?"

"I told you, they..."

"The *whole* story, please."

Damien swallowed, then nodded. "Okay, well..." It appeared that telling the unvarnished truth was indeed a very difficult task for him. "I travel around a lot like Ekko does, you know, and..."

"Leave me out of it," she sniped. "You won't get any sympathy that way. We aren't the same."

He bit back a retort and nodded. "Like I said, I travel. I live in Galantus most of the time because business is good there, but I'm actually from a little town near the region where Rosend, Ironshield, and Heavenly Skies all meet. It's a pretty dangerous area. Ironshield's soldiers are always raiding across both of the borders; that's actually one reason why I left."

"Go on," Daijera goaded. "There's clearly more to it than that."

"Yeah, so I stayed away from that area for a long time, but after Ekko and I, um, parted ways–" He shot a look at Ekko, and her expression was icy. "Well, I headed for home to try and lie low. I figured no one would look for me there. But I hadn't counted on how bad things had gotten. Ironshield soldiers were occupying a lot of the area around where my folks lived. So I snuck into town and stayed in the loft. My mom would bring me food, and I just generally kept out of sight. But then this different unit of soldiers showed up, and they were still Ironshield, but they were worse than the others. They were grabbing people from the village and taking them off in caged carts. They grabbed my mom, and when my dad tried to stop them, well...you can imagine." He paused, a haunted look passing over his face.

"Young man, I empathize heartily with you. I, too, watched my father be slaughtered by Ironshield soldiers." Dalgis couldn't help remembering how his father had been led up the gallows by the soldier with the crescent moon scar on his neck. Someday, Dalgis vowed, he would turn that crescent into a full moon and bleed the man dry. "What you have suffered is horrific. But that in itself will not win us over."

"I know, I know. Everybody's got a story," Damien grumbled. "But anyway, when they...you know...my father, I jumped down from the loft. I couldn't let them take my mother and my father from me on the same day. I hate to admit it, but I was no match for them, and they had me on the ground in seconds. But they couldn't decide whether to kill me or put me in a cart. Truthfully, I was half-dead already. There was this soldier in red armor...I never did see his face, but his helm looked like a lion. He seemed to be in charge. And they were discussing what to do with me when there was this huge explosion behind them. That's when Phelia and her Skulls showed up. She did some weird trick to project her voice, and she announced, '*You have taken all you need from this village, servants of the King! Be gone!*' and then it was the damndest thing you ever saw. The soldiers just rolled out. Like they were afraid of Phelia or something. They just left without another word, and there I was, bleeding in the dirt while my mother got carted away."

"So she saved your life?" Daijera asked. "That means you owe her a blood debt?"

"Something like that. She agreed to spare me if I would help her and the Obsidian Skulls. And I thought that they must be enemies of Ironshield, so I agreed."

"But now you don't think so?"

"NOW I THINK THE SOLDIERS just fear her. I don't think they're enemies exactly, because Phelia has that research base inside Ironshield's borders. At least that's where it is now. They move it every eleven months, I heard."

"And now you want to join us because you think we are Ironshield's enemies? Is that it?" Daijera pressed.

"Whether you are or not, you had her interest, so that means you've got some sort of pull. Otherwise she either wouldn't have bothered with you, or she'd have done something awful to you. So yeah, I think my best chance of escape is with you."

Daijera considered this, then looked at Ekko and Dalgis. Dalgis couldn't help being moved by the story, and figured that anyone who hated Ironshield, particularly a human who hated Ironshield, was worth helping.

"I'll tell you what, Damien," the lamia began, "your tale is a good one, but the full decision must go to our whole group. Here is what I propose: you prove your good faith to us by reporting Phelia's activities to us for the next couple of weeks while we run a little errand north of here. If you prove yourself trustworthy, we'll swing back through town and take you with us. Even then, you will be regarded with the highest scrutiny. But if you pass muster, we will see if we can find a way to throw Phelia off your scent. Do you accept those terms?"

He looked up, and something like hope flashed across his young face before his cynical expression returned. "I agree to your terms."

"Don't get too excited," she said as she turned toward the door in a flourish of hair and skirts. "I have strong doubts that the rest of the group will go along with it. But I will propose it on your behalf, and we will let you know before we leave town tomorrow."

"And," Dalgis added, "I still reserve the right to eat you if you betray us in any way." He was half kidding. But only half.

Chapter 9

Skyfire

Argus

Moraia had given them a general area on the map where the storm elves' capital city was located. But, she told them, they weren't likely to find the actual city unless the storm elves wanted them to. It was deep in the Salaam Mountains in northeastern Rosend; the name of the city was Talam, which translated to Skyfire, the storm elf word for lightning.

She also said that the elves would likely be watching the group as they traveled, sizing them up. Storm elves weren't inherently warlike, but they were fiercely protective of their territory and their privacy.

"If they make contact with you," she had said, "you'll have about fifteen seconds to make an impression. If you want them to take you to their city, you'll need to show the utmost respect. They need to know you're not a threat."

"So how do we do that?" Argus had asked.

"I have no idea. I never have to go through all those formalities. My association as a high priestess of Hohn affords me certain...privileges."

"How do we find the city if they don't make contact?"

"Oh, you probably won't. It's very well hidden."

"Can you, perhaps, give us a little more direction?" Argus tried to hide his growing frustration.

"I'm afraid not. I don't travel on foot as you'll be doing. On foot, I'm not even sure *I* could find it. But have faith! Hohn is with you!"

Moraia beamed at him, no doubt in her mind that the group would find their way. Argus wished he shared her optimism.

That had been three days ago. They had traveled north for a day, and that part had been easy, but then they had entered the mountainous area, and their pace had slowed dramatically. The air had a biting chill once the sun went down, and despite the warm clothes Colvyn had loaned them, Dalgis and Daijera seemed ill-suited to the cold.

On the afternoon of the third day, Dalgis nudged Argus as they walked single-file through a narrow pass between two massive hills.

"Pardon me, Argus," the beast said with somewhat less exuberance than usual, "but I thought you should know that I scented a number of people––elves, I'm almost certain, though their scent is a bit different than what I'm used to, and the cold may be interfering with my senses a bit—following us for the last three-quarters of an hour."

"That's good news, thank you, Dalgis," Argus replied, a sense of hope washing over him. "They're probably doing what Moraia said, watching to see if we're a threat."

"I do have a question, though. If they did see us as a threat, presumably they'd set up an ambush."

"Presumably, I concur."

"And if they do not see us as a threat, they would let us go on about our travels?"

"Yes, I should think so."

"Then how do we get them to take us to the city? If they don't see us as a threat, why would they even make contact?"

"Quite right, Dalgis. I had the same thought. I have been developing a plan since we started out this morning, and if they don't attack us before sundown, I have an idea. I'll share it with everyone when we set up camp."

"The sun should be setting in about two hours, I believe."

"Yes indeed, but I think the main thing is to get out of this pass and into a more open area if we can. Trying to camp in an area like this is just asking for trouble. We'd be hemmed in if they decide to attack."

Dalgis nodded. "I shall be quite happy to huddle near a fire well before sundown, if I'm being completely candid with you. I'm not cold-blooded like Daijera is, but I'm far better suited to more temperate climes."

Argus smiled. "Duly noted, friend. Stig isn't too happy, either, though he has weathered his share of Breadstone winters. As soon as we find a safer location, we can set up a nice campfire, maybe two."

"That is much appreciated." Dalgis drifted to the back of the line, where he had positioned himself so that he could protect the group from attacks from the rear.

Now that he knew the storm elves were watching, it was time to start the subtle parts of his plan to draw them out.

"Daijera," Argus called in a cheerful voice, "might you pull out your lute and sing to us as we walk along?"

"Is that an attempt at humor?" she called back.

"Certainly not. It appears that you may have a somewhat larger audience than what you can see, if you catch my meaning." Though she had quite a few faults, Argus felt certain that Daijera would see the larger picture and play along. Indeed, after a short pause, lilting notes from her instrument began to fill the air. It was a bit clumsier than her normal playing, but Argus surmised that that was because of the gloves she had donned to conserve her body heat.

The music continued for a few more minutes, and then she let her voice take the place of the lute. She had opted for a sad ballad about sailors lost at sea. It was, perhaps, not thematically appropriate, but the notes were haunting and created a surreal harmony when echoed back off the walls of the small canyon.

The path eventually opened out onto a small meadow. Tiny yellow flowers dotted the field, almost like a massive carpet across the valley.

To the left, a stand of trees stood in stark relief at the meadow's edge, and a tall, jagged peak climbed from behind the border they created. A gentle but large hill rose up on the right.

"I think this looks like a pretty good place to camp," called Ren from the front of the group. We only have about an hour of daylight left, and it will take us half of that to set up camp.

"Agreed. Let's set up our bunk sites in a circle around a firepit, shall we?" He didn't say so out loud, but Argus's motive for the suggestion had been in order to have a better fighting position, should it become necessary.

Once they'd arranged things, they gathered stones in order to make a fire pit. Ren pulled out his flint to light the kindling, but Argus stopped him. "Xezia, would you come help me start a fire, please?"

The mage moved forward, one eyebrow raised in confusion. But when Argus began the intricate hand movements of lightning magic, Xezia caught on immediately and followed suit.

The two men stood opposite each other and began to circle the pit, Xezia following Argus's hands precisely. Tiny tendrils of lightning began arcing between their fingers, controlled and beautiful in their precision. As their gestures became larger, so did the lightning, arcing now across the firepit from one man to the other. The others watched in silent fascination, and, unless Argus missed his guess, so did the hidden storm elves.

At the climax of the light show, Argus and Xezia stood with their arms wide, the crackling electricity forming a dome above them. Then Argus nodded and each brought his hands together in a mighty clap, and a sizzling bolt shot down from the clouds above, igniting the wood in the firepit. The flames blazed blue for an instant, then settled into a merry campfire.

Everyone gathered around to soak in the warmth while Argus sorted through his cooking gear. Dalgis curled around fully one half of the circle, warming one side of his massive body, and Daijera's eyes fluttered closed as she enjoyed the heat. Ekko, Elia, and Ren made small talk while Argus boiled water for tea and soup. Xezia surreptitiously searched the surrounding terrain for signs of the elves.

Once the tea was made and everyone was feeling comfortable, Daijera brought forth the lute again and sang a song in a sun elf dialect. By the time the song reached its conclusion, a newcomer stood solemnly outside their circle, silently watching, but no longer hiding his presence.

The storm elf stood a bit shorter than the sun, sand, and sea elves that were so commonly seen in the rest of Rosend. His skin was the color of charcoal, and stood in stark contrast to the shock of white hair cut in short, choppy layers and standing nearly straight out from his scalp. His black eyes regarded the party carefully, and his demeanor communicated that this contact could be the beginning of peace or battle.

No one said a word or moved as Argus poured the elf a cup of tea and handed it to him without speaking. Remembering Argus's stories about the silent meal, Dalgis fished a piece of fruit out of Ekko's bag and offered it to the stranger, who accepted it with a nod, and came to sit in the circle around the fire. Argus chopped vegetables and cured meat into pieces and tossed them into the hot water, and within a few minutes, he served soup to everyone.

At the end of the meal, the storm elf stood and bowed deeply, then turned and let out a piercing whistle. From hidden spots all around the perimeter of the meadow, two dozen storm elves emerged, their arms spread wide to show that they held no weapons. They formed a circle around the party, then laid down their gear and sat comfortably facing the fire.

Argus heaved a sigh of relief, and sent a prayer of thanks to his father for dragging a gangly boy along to trade grain for lumber so long ago.

Ekko

Just after sunrise, Ekko was jolted awake by a sharp *CLACK!* close enough and loud enough to be almost painful. She leapt to her feet, a dagger in each hand, prepared to defend herself or gut whoever chose to wake her up that way, whichever seemed the most appropriate.

When her eyes focused, she found herself staring at a female storm elf with ashen skin and snowy white hair. The elf was holding two stones in front of herself, shoulder-width apart. Seeing Ekko's alarm, she broke into tinkly laughter. She made a horizontal circling gesture toward the party's stirring bodies, who had been slower to wake. The elf grinned and slammed the rocks together again. This time, one by one, the group sat up, looking sleepy and confused.

"I believe that's a storm elf wake-up announcement," Argus commented over his shoulder at Ekko. He was over by the fire, as he always was before dawn, making hot tea to get the morning started. "You can put your weapons down, Ekko."

She hesitated before doing so. What would make anyone think that was an acceptable way to awaken fully-armed strangers? Nevertheless, she sheathed her daggers as the elf continued to shake with mirth.

It only took a few minutes for everyone to pack their gear, and while no one was looking, Ekko grew her thick orange fur beneath her clothes so she could keep warm for the rest of the journey.

For all their silence before, the elves were downright chatty now, as they led the way north. The elf with the tinkly laugh prattled on and on to Ekko, gesturing frequently at different flora and fauna and land formations as they hiked along. Ekko assumed that the young woman was trying to teach her the storm elf names for junipers, hills, and crows. Then she tapped Ekko's arm and said, "*Erfa.*"

"Erfa?" Ekko asked, pointing at herself. The elf nodded enthusiastically. "Erfa?" Ekko asked again, this time pointing at the elf, who shook her head.

"*Ralfa*," said the elf, indicating herself. Okay, so *erfa* didn't mean *female*.

"Erfa?" Ekko pointed at Argus.

"*Erko*," the elf corrected her.

"Erfa?" Ekko asked, pointing at Elia.

The elf looked over at the girl walking beside Argus and nodded. "*Erfa!*" She smiled broadly, as though Ekko had just become her prized student.

Okay, so *erfa* meant human female, and *erko* meant human male. That meant that *ralfa* must mean elf female, or maybe just storm elf female. Ekko wasn't sure how this would be at all useful, but it did make for a fun game as they walked along. By the time the first storm elf farmhouses were in sight–small, square buildings of mortar and stone with heavy wooden roofs–she had learned maybe 20 words in the storm elf dialect.

The farms themselves were nestled against the edge of a great mountain, its peak disappearing into the heavy clouds. Each farm had a small number of elves working with small shovels or knives, harvesting root vegetables or gourds. Without exception, the farmers stopped and watched the strangers pass by. Ekko wondered if these people had ever seen someone who *wasn't* a storm elf. They were known for their lack of interaction with the outside world, after all.

At the end of the line of farms, a thick forest filled what was left of the valley, and at the edge of this forest, the first elf, who Ekko had learned was called Gidón, held up a hand, indicating that the newcomers should wait at the woods' edge. He and a dozen of his scouting party disappeared into the trees. A few minutes later, Gidón returned alone, and beckoned for everyone else to follow him into the trees and, presumably, toward the elven city.

She wasn't sure what she was expecting, but there was no way Ekko could have imagined the sight that greeted her.

"*Talam!*" Ekko's new friend (whose name was Croia) beamed, pointing ahead. "*Foi na Talam!*"

Ekko had seen caves before, but nothing like this one. The entrance was far larger than any she'd seen before—more than fifty feet—with a small river burbling out of its center, leaving a walking path of fifteen or so feet on each side. On each side of the cave entrance, balconies had been cut into the stone, presumably for keeping watch and mounting defense. Each balcony looked as though it could hold a dozen archers if that became necessary, though now only two peered over the balcony's edge to watch Gidón's guests approach.

As they made their way deeper into the mountain, Talam, the city of the storm elves, rose up in front of them. Though the sunlight was weaker here, there was a dim greenish-blue glow cast by a chandelier of massive stalactites hanging from above, and the walls were inscribed with veins of crystal which glowed like arcs of lightning across the walls. Ekko's jaw hung open as she absorbed the beauty of the place.

Croia giggled and clapped when she saw Ekko's reaction, as though she were a child who had been given a surprise gift rather than an elven warrior. "*Nafala Talam!*" she announced, hugging Ekko around the shoulders.

"Nafala Talam," Ekko agreed.

Gidón led them up the narrow main street toward a large, three-story building in the center of the town. As they paraded down the thoroughfare, it seemed as though all other activity in Talam paused so the residents could come and ogle the procession.

Croia was thrilled to be in the middle of it all, and she linked arms with Ekko and waved at the onlookers. A high-pitched and chaotic roar of children's voices rose above the semi-quiet as seven gray and deep blue-skinned little ones rushed to the edge of the street, fascinated by the funny-looking people. Ekko's heart warmed at the sight of them. She had never much liked kids, but these seemed different somehow.

Maybe their fascination with her and her companions had won her over.

Argus and Gidón went inside the large building, leaving the rest of the group to wait in the small town square.

"Hey, why don't we entertain them while we're waiting?" Ekko suggested. Elia's eyebrows shot up in surprise, mirroring the sentiment on the faces of the others.

"Do what now?"

"Entertain them! I mean, they're all already staring, and we want to stay on their good sides, right?"

"What has gotten into you?" Xezia asked. "Since when do you volunteer to be a circus freak?"

"Oh, don't be a bore, Xezia. Look at them! They want to like us. Do some magic! Daijera, play your lute again!"

Xezia and Daijera looked at each other, then Daijera shrugged and pulled out her instrument. She began to play a cheerful and lilting tune with sharp, precise notes that echoed beautifully off the walls of the cavern. Xezia made a sour face.

In the center of the square, a gnarled and somewhat petrified tree reached upward like an aged and clawed hand. Ekko marveled at it, thinking it must have been fed by some underground rivulet of the river that wound through the cave. Birds flew in and out of the cavern, perching on thatched roofs and flower boxes, but none would land in the tree.

Something itched at the back of Ekko's mind. Flower boxes... birds...why was that important? A flash of blue caught her eye as a blue bird soared above their heads and down a residential street.

"Caa caa!" shrieked the bird as it flew by, attracting the attention of a lazy-looking feline that had been curled up on a rooftop. Sensing, perhaps, a satisfying dinner, the cat leapt up and chased the bird down the street, jumping from roof to roof until it was out of sight.

Suddenly, the memory clicked and Ekko ran to Xezia, punching him in the arm. His eyes widened at her boldness, then narrowed in annoyance. "Do some magic, you grouch! This is like Fufei's vision from Hohn! Hohn likes flowers! Make flowers!"

"Flowers? Are you daft? I–" Ekko cut him off by punching his arm again. Croia watched in utter confusion. "Oh, all right. Skies above. It's just going to be an illusion, mind you, but enjoy it."

He began muttering softly to himself, making strange gesticulations with his fingers. At the end of his spell, he popped his fingers upward, and the tree in the center of town erupted in pink and red blooms.

The crowd gasped, their mouths forming into tiny o's as they beheld the tree. Argus and Gidón appeared at an upstairs window with an older elven woman. Argus's expression was unreadable, but the elves' eyes were full of wonder.

Xezia blew a soft stream of air through his lips and an illusory breeze blew through the branches of the tree, lifting the blooms into the air and carrying them out to the crowd, where they dissipated like fresh snowflakes. When the last of the flowers were gone, the elves erupted into applause and cheering.

Croia, her eyes wet with tears, threw her arms around Ekko and hugged her, laughing like tiny bells. The feeling of wonder and joy hung thickly in the blue-tinted light.

Even Xezia smiled.

"*Hohn ma na keh!*" Croia wept aloud, and within seconds, cheers of "*Hohn ma na keh!*" echoed through the cavern.

Chapter 10

Goddess

Xezia

He couldn't explain it, but he could feel it reverberating through him.

Hope. Pure, warm, and pulsing through every fiber of his being. There was another feeling, too...one that was much harder for him to identify. The moment he had made the illusory wind blow illusory flowers around the cave, a wave of *something* had washed over him, and it seemed to originate from the faces and gasps of wonder erupting from the storm elves. Their eyes glowed and some of them had clutched at their hearts, not in pain or fear, but in...*joy*.

Joy. He felt joy.

How was this possible?

The flowers had begun to fade and disappear, but the mood in the town had not waned in the least. Citizens of Talam were grinning and hugging each other, and the children roared with laughter, trying to chase down the remaining blooms before they vanished.

In the middle of Xezia's existential crisis, Argus, Gidón, and the ancient elf woman emerged from the front archway of the white-washed wooden building that seemed to be the center of the town's activities. Argus beckoned for the group to gather around.

"Everyone, this is Olifa, Elder of the city of Talam. Olifa, these are my friends."

"My greetings to you, fair people. You honor our city with your presence." Olifa's skin was the color of ashes, but her eyes shone like the sky at midnight. She was only a few fingers taller than Ekko, but she walked with the presence of a giant.

"Oh! You speak Dyosa!" Elia gasped.

"Yes, young lady. The Elder of Talam must learn to speak all of the surrounding languages in case negotiating a treaty becomes necessary. I learned from my predecessor, and I am training the young man who will replace me one day." She turned her attention to Xezia, and the wrinkles around her eyes and mouth deepened as a glowing grin spread across her features. "You have brought smiles to my people this day. I thank you."

Traces of a smile still lingered on Xezia's lips. "It is my honor," he replied.

"Your friend Argus has told me of your quest," she said, addressing the entire party. "I do not know the location of the artifact you seek, but there is one among us who may be able to guide you. He has been the city's premier herbalist for as long as anyone can remember, and he may have some wisdom to share with you. His name is Solaris. Gidón will guide you to his shop, but I must prepare you. Solaris is a bit surly with outsiders, and I cannot promise he will be willing to assist you."

"Nevertheless, we thank you," Argus assured her. "Olifa has agreed to allow us to take up to two days' rest here in Talam, and has invited us to feast with the townspeople this evening after we've spoken to this Solaris fellow."

"You are most gracious, my lady," Ren smiled, bowing slightly.

"We are honored," Dalgis agreed, swishing his tail back and forth as children giggled and jumped over it as though it were the largest toy they'd ever seen (which, perhaps, it was).

Olifa chuckled at the sight of the children's game. "We will see you this evening, then." She turned crisply and retreated into the building.

Gidón clapped Argus on the shoulder and inclined his head toward a narrow side street to the right of the town hall. "Lead on," Argus nodded, and everyone marched along behind them, hoping that Solaris had something useful to tell them.

Solaris's shop was situated against the edge of the cave, backing up to the inside of the mountain. There was no glass in the small window next to the door of the shop, an unusual feature for a business. Perhaps, Xezia theorized, the interior of the cave was largely immune to the changes in weather because it was so far from the mouth of the cave.

"*Solaris! Nat ma hey! Rem dinaa erkan koi lev,*" Gidón called into the window as they approached.

"*Mag nanda lam,*" came a strong, but clearly very bothered voice from within.

Gidón shook his head with an indulgent smile, and pushed open the door. Shelves lined the wall of the shop, floor to ceiling, and each shelf held dozens of jars and potted plants. A figure was hunched over a pile of broken pottery, sweeping it up with a hand broom. "*Nat ma hey,*" Gideon said again, and the figure grunted in annoyance. "*Olifa rehan dolón.*"

The figure sighed and stood up. Xezia wasn't sure what he had been expecting, but it certainly wasn't the man who stood before them. Argus's brows rose slightly, and Xezia heard Daijera catch her breath. Olifa had said that Solaris had been in Talam for as long as anyone could remember, but he looked no older than 35. His skin was like a polished jet stone, and he positively radiated power. Even beneath the tunic he wore, his torso was visibly muscled and he looked much more like a royal guard than a shopkeeper. His black hair was neatly and tightly braided, adorned with silver rings, and his pale gray eyes regarded the group with profound disinterest. He sighed again and crossed his arms.

Out of the corner of his eye, Xezia caught Daijera dialing up her glamour in an attempt to appear more beautiful. Solaris's left eye twitched, and Xezia was pretty sure the unlikely shop owner had noticed as well.

"Gidón here tells me that Olifa wants me to talk to you," Solaris said flatly, "so out of respect for her position, I will grant you a little time. I assume you aren't here to buy herbs or tinctures."

"Well, we might, though you are correct that our errand is a bit more...complicated." Daijera smile was radiant, and though she was quite adept at her glamour magick, Solaris was completely unimpressed. He rolled his eyes slightly and turned to Argus, who was standing at Gidón's side.

"If Gidón led you here, then I assume your visit has some merit from their point of view, but please don't be misled. What may seem critically important to you is little more than a trifle to me. Ask me what you came to ask me so I can go back to the world-changing duty of sweeping up broken plant pots." Gidón, having accomplished his task, muttered something in the storm elf tongue and made a hasty exit.

Ignoring the evident irritation in his voice, Elia cried, "Oh, you speak Dyosa, too! We were under the impression that storm elves don't speak other languages, and now we've met two of you who we can talk to!"

Solaris didn't share her excitement. "Child, I have been to every corner of every land, and I speak more languages than you know exist. Why is it that such a mixed band has graced me with its presence?" His tone indicated that he didn't feel particularly graced at all.

Daijera seemed as though she were about to speak, but then snapped her mouth shut. Argus cleared his throat. "We won't take too much of your time, I hope," he began. "I can see that you're terribly busy." Solaris cast him a withering glare, but Argus plowed on. "We were guided to you, rather indirectly, by a high priestess of Hohn named Fufei, and then by another woman who I suspect is also a priestess of some sort. Her name is Moraia."

Solaris's eyebrows wrinkled slightly at the mention of the names, and it seemed that Argus had caught his attention. He opened his mouth to reply, but was interrupted by a chirpy voice.

"Oh, Moraia isn't a priestess. She's a Champion. She's very pretty."

Everyone spun around to find a child of about eight years old sitting comfortably on the window sill, swinging her legs. Her enormous puffy pink skirt covered the entire length of the window.

Xezia found himself quite unable to speak, his heart pounding in his chest so hard that he suspected everyone in the room could hear it. The amulet around his neck grew warm against his skin.

"Oh! Who are you?" Elia's eyes were as wide as moons. "You clearly aren't from here."

The child laughed, and it sounded like raindrops on bells. She tossed her golden curls and fixed her luminous blue eyes on Elia. "I'm from pretty much everywhere, Elia," she replied, and her demeanor was as genuine and friendly as Solaris's had been icy. "Don't let old Solaris scare you off. He's grumpy, but he has the purest of hearts. Don't you, Solaris?"

A low and frustrated-sounding growl erupted from the ancient elf's chest. "Hello, Epi," he grumbled. "I might have suspected you had something to do with this."

Xezia felt light-headed.

She was here.

His Goddess was here.

Daijera

Daijera had frequently asked herself why she was still tagging along with this luck-forsaken party of adventurers, and that sense of doubt was now quickly turning to an urge toward self-preservation. She slunk back against the wall in humiliation.

At first, the child had looked harmless, with her curls and ribbons bouncing as she skipped into Solaris's shop and hopped up on the windowsill. Never had a first impression been so wrong. Instead of a harmless child, they found themselves looking into the wide aqua eyes of Epi, Goddess of Purity.

Purity was never a virtue that had had much sway with Daijera. She sang in taverns, she hustled money from patrons, and she bartered information for the Black Moon when the opportunity arose. Thankfully, Epi's attention wasn't on her, so she inched her way to the back of the group and shut her mouth.

"I'll have you know that this was my Sister's doing, not Mine, Solaris, and you would do well to remember who you serve." She turned her attention from him and smiled brightly. "You all have been awfully busy," Epi said in her musical voice, "collecting Books and things. I thought it was time we met." She fixed her gaze solidly on Xezia. "And I believe you wanted to speak with me?"

Xezia cleared his throat and looked uneasily at the group. "Yes, my Lady. I was wondering if you could help with this?" He pulled off his gloves, and the veins of both forearms pulsed with Ebon Ichor in the place of blood.

Elia recoiled and stepped closer to Argus. "Whaaa...what is THAT?"

Daijera's eyes grew wide. She knew Xezia had been tricked and used by Ipthel, but she hadn't realized the extent of what was happening to him. She had thought the gloves were a fashion choice, perhaps even a symbol of his mourning. But even beyond the shock of seeing what had been happening to what was supposed to be her one guaranteed ally in the group, she began to worry even more about her own situation. What was Xezia doing?

Epi looked disappointed as she studied Xezia's arms. "I might have expected this. I can help you, Xezia, but I'm not sure you'll like the consequences."

"What do you mean?" he asked.

"I can help you, but you'll lose the use of any powers granted to you by Ipthel. If you use them, the corruption will return."

EVERYONE EXCEPT ARGUS and Solaris looked genuinely shocked. *Ipthel?*

Xezia nodded gravely, as though he'd expected this. "What if I were to serve You instead of Ipthel? Can you help me? Can you get Sora back?"

Daijera looked back and forth from Xezia to the tiny goddess. If Xezia were to serve Epi instead of Ipthel? Wasn't he a mage of Epi? Had he been lying all along and serving Corruption? And if he turned his alliances...if he turned on the Black Moon...what were the implications?

"I suppose that might help with your situation, but I can't promise anything about your friend until I find out what's happened to her. If she lives, I can find her for you," Epi replied, "but I suspect Ipthel won't be too happy with you. He's not likely to take your defection well."

"Do it," Xezia muttered.

The goddess nodded and took Xezia's hands in hers. A radiant light flowed out of her and crept up his arms, devouring the ichor as it went. He grimaced in pain, but made no sound.

While the party was focused on what was happening, Daijera began inching toward the door. If Xezia denounced Black Moon, could she trust his loyalty? Despite her rising concerns since Sora's disappearance, Xezia was the one person who she could probably trust to support her without question, if only because the Code of the Black Moon dictated it. If he had no Code, or worse, if he followed Epi's code of purity, Daijera would be alone. Again.

As she neared the door, she caught Solaris watching her not-so-stealthy retreat, and even with a sour expression on his face, she thought he might well be the most beautiful creature she'd ever seen. She smiled innocently and he raised a heavy eyebrow. She withered under his detached and somewhat disapproving glare, and she rebuked herself for being fool enough to hope that he might welcome her attention.

What was happening to her? Traveling with this motley band over the past few months had made her soft and desirous of personal connections, a weakness she'd never succumbed to in all her years. Even with her skill at glamour, her charm and performer's charisma, she would always be an outcast. Had her childhood taught her nothing?

A grunt from Xezia brought her attention back to the matter at hand. He knelt before the child goddess with a look of agony spread across his features. The formerly blackened veins glowed gold, then faded from view as Epi released her grip.

"Okay, now, Xezia," she began in the tone a child adopts when imitating a parent, "I have cleansed your spirit as much as I can, but I couldn't rid you of Ipthel's stain entirely. You must resist the urge to use the power He gave you. Anytime you indulge in it, the seed of corruption within you will grow again. It's like watering a dormant seed; do you understand?"

Xezia nodded, but stayed on one knee, too unsteady to stand. Epi patted his head as though he were an obedient pet. "I believe in you, Xezia." She kissed him on the cheek and his eyes glazed over in adoration.

"I always thought you ignored my prayers," he confessed. "I'm sorry for doubting you."

"I heard you, but it wasn't me you were praying to, not really," she soothed. "Ipthel saw to that with the mentors He sent into your path. But I'm here now."

Xezia nodded, tears standing in his eyes. She beamed at him for a moment, then turned to the rest of the group. Only Solaris seemed unmoved by the scene.

"My Sister tells me that you are collecting Books to stand against that rotten King Godfroy," she announced.

"Your Sister?" asked Dalgis, extending his head through the open window.

"Yes, my Sister Hohn," she chirped. "She has told me about you, too, Dalgis. You are just as marvelous as She described. What fun your father must have had designing you! I like these!" She reached out and petted his feathered frill.

"Hohn spoke to you about me?" Dalgis asked, gobsmacked.

"Oh, yes. She said you two had a lovely conversation a little while ago. She likes you."

Dalgis looked as though he might burst with pride and happiness.

"She told me you would find your way here eventually, so I've been keeping an eye on Solaris's shop. I suppose you intend to go get Her Book now?"

"That is, indeed, the plan, my Lady," Ren answered, "and I believe I speak for all of us when I thank You for honoring us with a personal visit."

"Oh, Sir Ren, you are so formal! I love it!" She skipped over to him and held out her arms to be picked up. Ren's eyes filled with panic and he scanned the group's faces for guidance. Did one pick up a Goddess? Epi wiggled her fingers insistently, and Ren bent down slowly and lifted her as though she were made of the thinnest porcelain. Epi giggled and tossed her curls, sending golden ringlets into his face as she turned to stick her tongue out at Solaris. The immortal elf rolled his gray eyes again. "Thank you, Sir Ren. Solaris won't *ever* pick me up."

"I'm afraid I'm unworthy of the title, my Lady, though I do appreciate Your courtesy."

"Don't be ridiculous, Sir Ren. I've never met a knight with a heart as pure as yours. I'm a bit of an expert on the subject, you know."

"On knighthood?"

"No, silly, on pure hearts. Obviously."

Ren looked stunned, and Daijera thought about the story he had told her. She smiled at the Goddess of Purity and silently thanked her for easing Ren's guilt.

Epi snapped her attention to Daijera and practically glowed with happiness. "Oh! You're welcome! You've never done that before!"

Daijera twitched, startled by Epi's reply to the words she had only thought. But Epi was a goddess after all, and people talked to Deities all the time in prayer. *Did I just PRAY?* Daijera wondered.

You most certainly did, Epi's voice answered in Daijera's head. *And don't worry about stupid old Solaris. He's handsome, but he's no fun. You wouldn't love him for long, I'll bet. The world is wide, Daijera. Find someone who appreciates you.*

Daijera's eyes grew wide, and her jaw hung open. Epi giggled and clapped her hands together, causing Daijera's long black hair to braid itself. A shiny pink ribbon appeared and tied itself into a bow at the bottom.

"Alright, my new friends, I think it's time you got going. My sister's demesnes are a bit challenging to navigate, but I have faith in you! And on the bright side, if you can't make it, it's likely Godfroy's people wouldn't either."

"Is that a vote of confidence?" Ekko asked. "I can't tell."

"I mean, I believe you can make it, but it's not my realm, after all. If you do make it, though, I'm sure our paths will cross again. Elia, when you all return to Solaris's shop here, check your bag. You'll find a letter from me there. Now off you go! Sir Ren, you may put me down over there on the counter." Ren obliged, and Epi nodded at Solaris. "You can let them in now."

Solaris sighed heavily. "Alright. This way. And you," he pointed at Dalgis, "walk around the left side of the building. I'll let you in the back way. The door is...different...there." He pulled back a curtain and headed into the back room of the shop, assuming everyone else would follow. The back room appeared to be his living quarters; there was a small bed, a desk, and a sizable cabinet. It had all the accoutrements, but it didn't feel *lived in*. The room itself backed up to the mountain, and no rear wall had been built. It simply flowed into the stone of the inner cavern.

Solaris approached the rear back corner, where Dalgis was supposed to be waiting on the other side of the wall. Then he mumbled a few quiet words and slammed his palm against the rock. The entire corner of the room shimmered and grew hazy, then disappeared, revealing a cave two Dalgises wide leading deeper into the mountain.

"Well, isn't that something!" Dalgis cried, stepping past what was left of the wall and sauntering into the cave's mouth. "Absolutely marvelous!"

"Good luck, everyone!" Epi called. But when Daijera looked back, the pink, the gold, and the curls were all gone.

Chapter 11

The Way and the Wall

Elia

"So, um, Solaris?" Elia asked as she began to step into the cave entrance. "I assume you can't just keep this portal open, right?"

The Champion rolled his eyes. "Obviously not."

"How do we get back? Will a doorway or cave or something just open up when we're ready to leave?"

"That would be ridiculous. The alternate reality you're entering bows to Hohn's will, not yours."

Elia felt her irritation rising. "How do we return, then?"

"How should I know? When I want to return, I just whisper an incantation in Hohn's language, and then I dematerialize there and rematerialize here."

"Can you teach us the incantation?"

"Are you asking if I *can* or if I *will*?"

"I don't know...both?" She wondered if Hohn would understand if she kicked his champion in the shins.

"I *could*, given enough time, but I'm not *going to*," he sniped. "This is your test, not mine."

"What do you mean *test*?" Ekko chimed in.

"Skies above, can you all do nothing for yourselves? However did you make it this far? You have to prove your worth. She's not just going to hand you Her Book."

"Ugh...more riddles?" Ekko whined. "I hated Utrui's temple. It gave me the worst headache."

"That's no surprise. Utrui's energy would run counter to yours, clearly. I don't have any idea what you'll be facing, and I wouldn't tell you if I did. The entire place is a manifestation of Hohn. Remember that. Now go, or I'll close the cave with you on this side of it."

"He really is a grump; Epi was right," Ekko remarked, grabbing Elia by the hand and dragging her after the others. Elia made a mental note to give Solaris a piece of her mind about treating people with courtesy when...if...they got back.

The cave stretched on for at least a mile, or so it seemed. It was hard to tell. The walls seemed almost alive; glistening veins of quartz cast an eerie glow, much like the illumination in Talam, but then the veins would turn to vines that visibly crept up the walls. The vines sprung to life with yellow and white flowers, and then the flowers would morph into butterflies and flutter toward the distant speck of light that appeared to be the far end of the passage. The constant and random cycle of change was fascinating, but also disorienting.

By the time they reached the mouth of the cave, the others stood in the small clearing, waiting.

"It's about time," Xezia sneered, but then caught himself. "Sorry. We, uh, seem to have very little direction as to which way to go, so that's what we were talking about when you joined us."

Elia raised an eyebrow and exchanged glances with Ekko. An apology? That had to be an Epi miracle if ever there was one.

The clearing was indeed small, only barely enough for all of them to fit comfortably. At its edge, nature was at its most primeval, combining jungle and forest in a tangled knot of flora all around them.

A test, Elia thought. *He said it was all a test.*

She began to walk around the perimeter of the clearing while Argus, Xezia, and Dalgis proposed various suggestions of how to proceed.

"Well, we could use a sword to cut the brush, of course," Argus offered, "but somehow, it seems that might be disrespectful to the Goddess."

"I do agree, Argus," said Dalgis. "Perhaps, being that I have significant girth and thicker skin, I could forge a path and you all could follow behind?"

"That's a good suggestion, Dalgis, but how would we know which direction to go? There must be clues to lead us..." Xezia was studying the trees, looking for some sort of writing or other indication of the correct path.

Elia was half listening to them as she ran her hands across the barks of trees that would never grow together in an ordinary setting.

The entire place is a manifestation of Hohn. Remember that.

Perhaps Solaris had been doing more than issuing a warning. He might be surly, but he DID serve Hohn. Epi had reminded him of that. So maybe he was helping in his grouchy way?

If everything around them was a manifestation of Hohn, then surely she was omnipresent here. It was Her domain, but it was also HER. What would one normally do if one needed help while visiting another person? The answer seemed too obvious to work, but it was worth a try, and somehow it seemed like exactly what Epi would do in this situation.

"Excuse me, Hohn?" Elia called, and Argus and Xezia turned sharply in her direction, each wearing a face one might reserve for a toddler banging pans together. "Um, hi! We made it! Would you be so kind as to show us which way to go and clear a path?"

Xezia snickered, "I suppose you had to at least try..." he began, but just then a breeze blew through the trees, and the rustling sounded a bit like laughter. Three archways of tangled roots sprung up from the ground, creating a way forward, but also a choice. Xezia's mouth hung open.

"It's always polite to ask," Elia smiled smugly. "That seems to have solved part of the problem, but which way should we go now?"

"If I may, Elia," Ren began, "I might suggest that you should make the choice. It was to your request that the Goddess responded, after all."

The rest of the group nodded in agreement, and Elia sighed deeply and went to examine the three paths before them.

The first path was dark and wound into a dense forest, and would be a bit of a tight fit for Dalgis. The branches above were so entangled that very little light seeped through to the ground. Still, the ground seemed hard-packed and easy to traverse, as though many had trodden the path before. There was no way to tell exactly where it went, but it looked safe enough, and Elia had a sense that no harm would come to them despite the darkness.

The second path was fairly well lit, and the ground was carpeted with soft green grass, though there were quite a few rocks they'd need to avoid so as not to turn an ankle. The trees here were stout and strong, and some were covered with a thorny ivy dotted with tiny purple flowers. The plants were unfamiliar and, Elia thought to herself, even her time in the herbalist's shop in Breadstone would not help her to know which ones were poisonous. Still, something about the path was familiar in a backwards way. She closed her eyes, and was flooded with a childhood memory of being snuggled close in Aunt Mita's arms. She imagined she could smell the lilac water Aunt Mita used to use to wash her hair. When she opened her eyes, the smell was gone, replaced by the acrid scent of burning wood.

The third path seemed to be an extension of the clearing, with the jumbled and mismatched plant life lining the sides, vibrating with life. Unseen birds chirped in the branches above, and fruit trees filled the air with the scents of apples, oranges, and mangoes. Dragonflies and fireflies danced in the branches, creating an illusion of arms dancing with movement. It was impossible to see which way the path went past about 40 feet, but it wound to the right and the ground was dappled with sunlight. She couldn't see them, but Elia had a sense of woodland creatures going about their business amongst the trees, and the path filled her with serenity.

"So which way?" Daijera prodded, but she didn't seem particularly impatient.

Elia looked at the three paths again, considering carefully. "This one," she decided, pointing down the center path.

"Why that one?" Ekko asked. "They all look pretty much the same to me."

"The same? They don't look alike at all!" Elia protested.

"To us, they all look the same, Elia," Argus replied. "A red, clay path lined with oak trees, disappearing into darkness in about twenty feet." Ren and Xezia nodded in agreement.

"It appears that this really *is* your decision, Elia," Ren said. "What made you select that path?"

She described the paths that she saw, and each of them agreed that the visions were hers alone. "I think it has to be the second path, because, well, the third path is far too inviting. It looks like everything will be easy. But if I've learned anything these last couple of months, it's that none of this is going to be easy. Anything that looks that inviting, that tempting, is probably a distraction or a trap."

"We'll make a cynic of you yet," Xezia chuckled, "but why not the first path? That seemed dark and uncertain, much like our mission, wouldn't you say?"

"Yes, I thought of that," she answered. "But Hohn wouldn't urge us to a dark path, I think. Especially not you, Xezia, since Epi is trying to bring you back to the light. And the path was also well-traveled, but no one has tried to do what we're doing, so that shouldn't be the case.

"The second is by far the most dangerous, but there are parts of it that call out to me, like I'm supposed to be there, like I'm supposed to face those dangers. And you, too, of course," she added quickly, so they wouldn't think that she was focused only on herself.

"Then the center path it is," Argus announced. "If that's the one that calls out to you, then we put our faith in you to lead us forward."

As he spoke, the other two root archways drew themselves slowly back into the ground, leaving no trace of their paths behind.

Elia was suddenly filled with panic. *What if I chose wrong? What if I lead them all into failure, or worse? What if my choice strands us here or costs someone their life?*

The thoughts flashed unbidden through her mind, but the fears and doubts she felt weren't reflected on the faces of her comrades. Their trust in her decision didn't erase her own fears, but it gave her strength.

Elia took a deep breath and squared her shoulders, then painted a confident grin across her face, as convincing as any of Daijera's glamours. "Onward, then," she said, only the lightest waver in her voice. "We have work to do."

Dalgis

Dalgis hummed discordantly as he followed along behind Elia. Well, it was discordant to the others, perhaps, but to his ears, he was humming along with the song of the flowers. It was a variation on one of the themes he remembered from his soothsayer tea vision, and it filled him with hope and a sense of belonging. It made him feel unique and special that no one else seemed able to hear the music.

He also felt like Elia had done a marvelous job leading them thus far, but it seemed wrong to have one so small leading into unknown and potentially dangerous territory.

"I say, Elia my lass, might I suggest that I take the forward position in the party? I'd hate to see you come to harm should an unexpected danger arise. I'm much more difficult to damage." She hesitated in her steps, and at first he was afraid he might have offended her, but then she beamed at him over her shoulder.

"That would be much appreciated, Dalgis. While I don't mind being in front, I feel as though I have to walk much more quickly than is comfortable, and I'd love to slow down for a little while."

"It would be my pleasure to lead in your stead for the moment." Dalgis bowed slightly in a gesture of respect for her leadership, and she glowed at the validation. She hugged his leg and dropped back toward the middle of the group, slowing her steps to a more comfortable pace. Dalgis surveyed the path for potential threats and saw none, but the road was a winding one, and the forest was continuously changing, as though they were traveling through many lands and climes.

After many minutes, the flowers' song rose to a trilling sound, as if in gentle warning, and Dalgis motioned for the group to slow their pace.

"Do you see something, Dalgis?" came Ekko's voice from behind him.

"Nothing yet; just a sense that something may be amiss." He didn't mention the flowers' warning because he wanted to focus on protecting his friends, but he made a mental vow to explain it to everyone later.

As he rounded the next bend in the path, the reason for the warning became clear. Cutting through the dense forest and growing directly across the path, a high hedge of thorns arrested their forward progress. The vines were densely woven together, and the thorns varied in size from the size of a child's tooth to the size of a man's thumb. All appeared to be barbed and razor sharp.

"OH, MY!" EXCLAIMED Dalgis. "It seems we have a bit of an obstruction."

Ren stepped forward, drawing his sword. "I seem to recall that swords are quite effective against jungles." He examined the thorny vines, looking for a spot that might give minimal resistance. He raised his sword to strike, and the shrill screams of the flowers assaulted Dalgis's sensitive ears.

"Wait, Sir Ren! Wait!" he cried, and the would-be knight stopped in mid-swing.

"Good heavens, Dalgis! What is it?"

"I, um, I think Hohn doesn't want you to do that."

"Please explain that statement," said Xezia, crossing his arms.

"Well, you see, I meant to bring this up later, but I suppose there's no time like the present, and well, I...I can hear the flowers. And they were very upset that you were going to do that."

"You can hear the flowers?" Xezia's eyes scrunched up in skepticism.

"I know how it sounds, Xezia," Dalgis protested. "But it's just like it was in my vision, you know? The flowers create music here, and I can hear it. And, well, imagine several high harp strings breaking at once. That's what I just heard."

"If Dalgis says he hears the flowers, then he hears the flowers," Ekko called petulantly from the back.

"Thank you, Ekko. Anyway, I feel like cutting the vines would be certainly insulting, and maybe even painful to Hohn. I believe we should find another way."

Ekko came trotting up to the front, making sure to shoot Xezia a dirty look as she went by. "I could try to climb it! I'm pretty good at climbing."

"I would imagine you are quite excellent at climbing," Dalgis replied, "but unless we can *all* climb it, I'm afraid that solution won't work. And despite the fact that I'm a fairly skilled climber myself, I don't believe I can make it without significant injury."

"What do you suggest?" asked Argus.

"Let us examine the vines closely. Perhaps some of them can be untangled, like a knotted skein of yarn, thus allowing us to pass through." Each of them chose a section of the hedge to examine, carefully taking hold of vines and attempting to unravel the twisted mess. But after nearly half an hour and several minor puncture wounds, they all had to agree that there was no getting past the wall that way.

"Maybe Elia led us down the wrong path," Xezia offered, earning himself another dirty look from Ekko. "What? It's a logical conclusion. We may well have been walking in the wrong direction for over an hour."

"I don't think so. I don't think the flowers would have been so cheery and musical if we were going the wrong way," Dalgis said, defending Elia.

"Well, then, why don't you ask your flower friends for some help? Are they not on speaking terms with the thorns?"

"There's no need to be mean, Xezia," Argus cut in. "But the point stands. Dalgis, might the flowers be able to offer some assistance?"

Despite his usual even-temperedness, Dalgis felt his frustration rising. The flowers had fallen silent, leaving him to solve the riddle on his own. He knew that they should not hack the vines down, and that he could not climb them. He knew that they could not go around them or pull them aside. He felt helpless, as though he were failing his friends, and the feeling struck a chord of memory.

From a distant treeline, he watched as the soldier with the crescent-moon scar on his cheek dragged his father toward the makeshift gallows the soldiers had built using a chair and some rope from the barn. Dalgis was so small then, only a few months old and barely the size of a wild turkey. His father had made him promise to stay hidden, no matter what, so he watched, not fully understanding what was happening, but knowing that it was bad, and that his father was in danger.

Several soldiers stood around, swords drawn, watching the woods carefully. Watching for Dalgis.

"Where is the abomination, wizard? Turn him over to the king, and you might yet walk away with your life."

Yussef Gomestible spat at the soldier's feet. "I'll tell you nothing, you swine. I have sent him far from here and you shall never find him."

"We'll just see about that, old man," the soldier sneered, forcing Yussef to stand on the chair and then looping the rope around the wizard's neck.

Dalgis trembled with terror. He must do something, no matter the cost! He must protect his father! He stepped forward, preparing his little body to run at the five soldiers with their angry blades, but suddenly his father's eyes found his, and he shook his head almost imperceptibly.

No, my son, said Father's voice in his head. You cannot save me from them. You are my joy and my legacy. Run away from here. Do not watch what happens next. Remember that I–

...and then the soldier kicked the chair out from under Yussef's feet, and the voice in Dalgis's head fell silent. He wailed as if he soul were being ripped apart, and then fled into the woods, swearing in his heart that when he got bigger, he would find the man with the crescent moon scar and make him suffer. And then he would find this new king of Ironshield and rip him from throat to belly.

The memories flooded Dalgis, emotions washing over him that he had buried deep within him. Why would Hohn thrust this challenge upon him, pulling his most painful memories to the surface? Why? Hadn't She told him he was Hers? On impulse, he ran at the wall of thorns, throwing all of his weight against it in an effort to punch through or to bring it down, as if doing so could make up for the time he had run away so many years ago. He flailed against the wall, the thorns tearing into his thick skin. He could hear Ekko's desperate cries behind him, begging him to stop, her hands pulling uselessly on his tail.

Everywhere in the thorny hedge that his claws had ripped through regrew instantly, and the tangled web of flora refused to yield. At last he stopped struggling, and became aware of two small bodies, Ekko and Elia, leaning against him and weeping.

"I'm sorry, friends," he muttered, his voice cracking with his own grief. "I only see one solution, and it may mean that you will return without me. I shall lean against the thorns, holding them down for you so that you may climb over safely."

"Dalgis, no!" cried Ekko.

"Surely there must be another way," Daijera said softly, using one of her scarves to try and dab at the blood running down his chest.

"No, my lady, there is no other way. If I turn my back to the thorns and lean against them, I can help you all to climb over. You must leave me behind. Perhaps Hohn will see fit to help me find my way back to you."

"We can't leave you!" Elia sobbed. "We have to stick together."

"I shall stay with you, my friend," offered Ren, placing a hand gently on Dalgis's shoulder.

"No, sir knight, you must protect our friends in my absence. Please, you must."

Ren's eyes were moist, but he nodded solemnly.

Despite the pain from several deep gashes left by the thorns, Dalgis gently pulled the girls off of him and stood to his full height. He gritted his teeth together and braced against the pain of dozens of thorns piercing his back. He took a deep breath and leaned into the hedge.

And the vines parted and retracted, disappearing into the forest, leaving no trace that they had ever been there other than the wounds in Dalgis's chest, arms, and heart.

Chapter 12

The Key and the Bear

Ekko

They had been walking again for a few minutes when Ekko caught up to an unusually quiet Dalgis. She punched him in the leg.

He turned to her, his expression quizzical. "And how should I interpret that?" he asked. He was rather polka-dotted, since Elia had covered him with herbal plasters to help his puncture wounds heal.

"I'm mad at you," she pouted. "You were going to just abandon me."

"I wasn't abandoning you, Ekko. I was doing what I had to in order to ensure your safety and the mission's success."

"So you say, but we might have still found another way. You gave up."

"I think that was the point." His eyes became momentarily unfocused, as though he were reliving a memory as he waxed philosophical. "I think Hohn wanted me to understand that sometimes aggression isn't the correct way to deal with a problem. Sometimes you must surrender and have faith."

Ekko shot him an angry look and crossed her arms.

"I shall tell you a secret, young Ekko. Before I charged the wall, I was remembering the time when I was unable to protect my father. If I had charged in to try and save him, we both would have been killed, and he knew that. So he told me to run. I knew I had no choice, but my heart has always been filled with regret for what I saw as my own cowardice in that moment. Today, I was in my father's shoes. He sacrificed himself to save me because he loved me. And I was willing to sacrifice myself to save you because I love you. I would have no regrets, and would bear no ill will toward any of you for leaving me to my fate. I think Hohn wanted me to let go of that regret from my past. Do you understand?"

"I guess," she retorted, smacking his leg again, but she was no longer angry, not really. Mostly she was uncomfortable that she had grown to love someone...again...whom she might have lost.

"Please know that I would not hesitate to give my life for you, Ekko. For any of you," he gestured at the group, "but mostly for you, little fox."

Why was he always so good at making her feel all gooey inside? "Please try not to let your nobility get the better of you," she grumbled, but then pet the spot where she had punched him.

He grinned. "That is a tall order from one so tiny, but I shall try."

She snorted, but she was sure he knew she was pretending to still be mad. She dropped to the back of the group so she could brood without his cheery disposition messing it up.

The path twisted along through the dense woods, and as they rounded a bend, it seemed to pass through a short tunnel of rock. Ekko looked up and saw a large, rusty-colored stone formation cutting through the trees. It somewhat resembled a narrow table, with the tunnel opening mimicking the space between the table's legs. It rather reminded her of a shape a child might make with clay.

The tunnel itself wasn't very long: maybe 40 feet, but it was brightly lit by sunshine coming in from either side. She heard the party *ooh*-ing up ahead, and by the time she entered the tunnel's mouth, she saw why. Veins of quartz and gold created elaborate patterns along the inside, all the way from end to end.

The amount of money reflected in these veins of gold ore was astounding, and Ekko ran her fingers longingly along one of them as she walked slowly through the passage.

I wonder if Hohn would be really mad if I chipped some of this gold out of the rock? she thought to herself. *I mean, it's not like She needs it, and I doubt she'd begrudge me taking a little to compensate myself for all I've been through, right?*

Deep down, Ekko knew she was rationalizing, and that she shouldn't use her dagger like a tiny pickaxe.

But it was So. Much. Gold.

The internal struggle was agonizing.

The vein she was tracing grew wider until it was the width of her entire hand. Even raw, the metal felt warm and reassuring against her palm, like the feeling of never risking being hungry or cold. She stopped and stared at it as the argument within her raged.

A tiny movement caught her eye, and she snapped her head to look at a spot in the vein maybe two yards back. As she watched, the gold seemed to be moving, forming itself into a shape. Slowly, the shape became familiar: a key with a round coin-like formation at the top and three notches at the bottom. She wasn't sure how, but she knew it was a house key. A solid gold house key as big as her longest finger. She reached out to touch it, and it dropped into her hand, glowing in the soft sunlight.

I guess Hohn DOES recognize that I deserve something for my trouble, she smiled to herself.

No one had noticed that she had dropped behind a little. She took a quick peek to make sure none of them were looking, and slipped the golden key into her pocket.

She might be willing to fight for at least some of the people walking ahead of her, but if she had learned anything in her young life, it was that you have to make sure to take care of yourself, because even people who claim to love you might not always be there.

Ren

The terrain in Hohn's domain was the strangest he'd ever encountered. That is to say, the overlapping melange of terrains was odd. One minute, they would be walking through mountainous land dotted with pines, and the next, they'd be seeing desert rock formations in the middle of dense rainforest. It made no sense at all.

But, he supposed, it wasn't for a mortal creature to tell a Deity how to decorate Her home.

He strolled along behind everyone else, watching their rear flank. Ekko was sprawled out on Dalgis's back, Argus and Xezia were in deep conversation, Daijera (looking remarkably peaceful for once) hummed as she walked, a bouquet of wildflowers in her hands which she was adding to every few minutes. Elia was nibbling on a honeycomb she had fished out of the snack stash in her pouch.

The animals here were an interesting mix as well. Squirrels, lizards, and birds were to be expected in nearly any environment, but it was quite surprising when a tower of giraffes wandered through with that ambling gait that made it look as though their heads were very precariously balanced atop their long necks. It was equally surprising to see an enormous yellow roc fly through the sky, screeching as it headed for its nest, carrying a deer in its talons.

So when Ren caught movement off to the right side of the path, he was alarmed, but not shocked, to see an enormous bear with grizzled brown and gray fur eyeballing the party from maybe twenty yards away. What was shocking was that no one else seemed to notice it.

"Hey, Bear!" Ren had been taught that, when passing through bear territory, one should make loud noises because bears would generally avoid confrontation with humans. "Hey, Bear!" The rest of the group paid no mind to his hollering, or to the beast that was sniffing the air, perhaps sizing up the herd of strange, two-legged creatures strolling through its meadow.

"Friends!" he called out. "You might wish to draw your weapons in case it decides to attack!" He drew his own sword, but everyone else carried on as if he hadn't spoken.

The bear, however, was quite aware of him. It stood up on its hind legs, and Ren judged it to be just over nine feet tall. The creature threw its head back and roared, a fearsome sound that frightened a flock of birds out of the nearest tree. It swept its gaze over the group, apparently considering its next action.

And then it spotted the small young woman near the back of the walking order, her hands sticky with honey.

The bear turned its attention back to Ren and roared again, and this time, its eyes flooded with darkness, the irises turning completely black. The darkness in its eyes spread across its face, dying the fur black and giving the illusion, just for a moment, that the creature had a void instead of a face. It dropped back onto all fours and broke into a run, heading straight for Elia at alarming speed. Each thundering step brought it closer, and Ren sprang into action. He ran toward the completely oblivious girl, brandishing his sword and yelling a warning, but she never even looked in his direction.

The bear was unbelievably fast, and Ren was unsure he would be able to get to Elia before the beast did, so he changed his course to intercept the bear directly. Why weren't the others attacking as well? They could easily have swept her out of the way. Xezia or Argus could have thrown fire or lightning at the bear from a distance. Why weren't they reacting?

Just as Ren reached the point of intercept, the bear altered its course and leapt toward him, its massive right claw slashing at him. The pad of its paw was the size of Ren's head, and the massive six-inch claws grazed his shoulder plate, knocking him off balance. His sword flashed in the sunlight as he swung it toward the hulking animal, but he misjudged the distance and only managed to make a small cut along its left shoulder. Then he leapt backwards as the bear swung its maw around, its upper lip curled back to try and take a bite.

Following the bear's earlier example, Ren closed the distance, smashing his other shoulder plate into the side of the bear's head, saving himself from the elongated canines, but the move came at a cost. The beast threw its weight forward, nearly knocking the knight to the ground. Then, with him off balance, it swept one claw across his ribs, sending him flying sideways into a tree.

HIS LEATHER ARMOR HAD provided him some protection, but he could feel the sting along his ribs, and the wetness of blood seeping through his tunic.

Seeing its opponent on the ground, the bear turned back to its original target: Elia. It struck Ren as strange that, even now, none of his compatriots had come to his aid, but as the thought crossed his mind, he raised his head to see the bear barrelling toward her. At the very last second, she looked up and her eyes filled with terror.

Ren struggled to rise, using the tree as leverage and then, ignoring the pain, ran toward Elia as the bear crashed its head into her. She sailed through the air, landing on her back several feet away. Shaking its head and gnashing its teeth, the bear loomed over her. Her scream rent the air, and at the sound, the rest of the group turned around in alarm.

Ren barely registered their surprised cries or the fact that he could hardly feel his left arm as he raised his sword and leapt at the creature, intending to impale it through the lungs in one downward strike, hoping that would at least allow Elia enough time to escape. He was fueled by pure adrenaline as he leapt high enough to plunge his sword downward.

The blade found the soft tissue between the bear's ribs, and with Ren's weight behind it, the sword sank through to its pommel. The grizzly let out a yowl and collapsed onto its side. It twitched once, then went still. Despite the pain in his side and the dizziness from loss of blood, Ren couldn't help thinking that killing the beast had been too easy. Even a wound as grave as the one he had just dealt should not have killed instantly in a beast like this one.

Still, he turned his attention to Elia as he sank to one knee. "Are you injured, my lady?"

"N-n-n-o," she replied. "Perhaps a few bruises, but nothing more. "But Ren!" She stared at the red stain that covered much of his left side.

"Where in the world did that bear come from?" came Ekko's voice from behind him as the rest of the group rushed forward.

"It was there in the meadow," Ren replied. "It must assume that this is Hohn's doing, as none of you were able to see it, or even hear us fighting until Elia screamed."

"Why would Hohn do this?" Elia asked, her eyes full of tears. "Ren, you saved me."

"It is my duty and my honor." Ren lay down on the grass, breathing heavily.

Daijera pulled some cloth from her bag and stepped forward. "Elia, do you have any of that salve left? We need to bandage him up before he loses any more blood." She deftly unbuckled his armor and tore the side of his tunic open, revealing several gashes which were bleeding significantly, but were not deep enough to be life-threatening.

Elia fished out the medicinal herb salve and set it next to Daijera, who was applying pressure to the wounds with one of the clean cloths.

"I deduce that Hohn is testing each of us in turn." Dalgis stepped up beside Daijera, his eyes full of concern. "And my friend, I have no doubt that you have passed by a wide margin. That was an incredible show of heroism."

Ren smiled wanly at Dalgis. "I have no doubt that any of you would have done the same."

Argus stepped up to the bear's body. "Perhaps, Sir Ren, but it is you who did."

Though somewhat embarrassed by the praise, Ren felt a wave of contentment wash over him. Though he had fought many battles in his life, this was the first time that he seemed to claim at least a temporary victory in the battle within himself.

"Something's happening." Xezia had joined Argus in inspecting the bear. Ren raised his head slightly so he could see, and as he watched, the fur and the flesh of the bear seemed to dessicate and then disintegrate. In less than a minute, only the skeleton remained.

Sitting within the rib cage, a tiny clay-colored bear cub sat trembling, not from fear, but from the awkwardness of being "born".

"Well, *that's* unexpected," Ekko proclaimed.

The cub blinked and looked around at the group, its slate-colored infant eyes searching each face in turn. At last, it met Ren's gaze, and made a soft squeak. Then it stood weakly on its new legs and stumbled in his direction. Everyone stood in guarded silence as it sniffed the wounded knight.

Then, seemingly satisfied, it gave a tiny but mighty yawn, curled up along Ren's unbandaged right side, and they both promptly fell asleep.

Chapter 13

The Vase and the Treehouse

Daijera

Daijera sat next to Ren as he slept, the bear cub still nestled close beside him. She ran her fingers idly over blades of grass that were stained red with blood. Was it Ren's or the bear's? It was impossible to be sure, and it probably didn't matter. Hohn would make the rain wash it away when She was good and ready.

Somehow, she had managed not to get much blood on her clothes as she tended and bandaged Ren's wounds, and she was glad for that. Blood stains had a habit of never washing away completely, and finding a new travel outfit would have been inconvenient.

She looked over at her sleeping friend–were they friends? She supposed so–and saw that he was breathing more easily than he had been. She reached over and peeked under the bandage, confirming her suspicion that Hohn was accelerating the healing process. After a solid nap, Ren would probably be fit to travel again, even if he was still a bit sore.

It was a bit disconcerting to her how detached she felt. Daijera had become quite fond of Ren, as she hadn't known too many men with principles in her life. He was reliable and honorable, and that was a refreshing combination. And yet, she hadn't been overly worried about his injuries. She would have liked to believe it was because she had faith that Hohn wouldn't kill him, but she suspected that the malaise that she had been feeling had been driving her to reconstruct the walls she had historically kept between herself and other people. After all, it was easier to leave people if you didn't let yourself love them.

Satisfied that Ren would be unconscious for awhile longer and that the group was content to let him sleep, she stood up and began wandering through the meadow, stopping here and there to add wildflowers to the bouquet she'd been gathering. Despite the melancholy that had been building in her, she liked it here in Hohn's demesnes. While she had felt miserable in Utrui's neatly ordered temple, the chaos of this untamed wilderness filled her with serenity. There was no limitation on how Nature might shape itself here, and rules only applied if Hohn Herself chose to honor them (which she often didn't).

Perhaps that was what drew Daijera to the wildflowers. Some were familiar, and some were not. Some were varieties she knew, but in colors that they never exhibited in the outside world.

She particularly liked the blue daisies: deep cobalt petals around summer-sky colored discs. She spotted a bush of them near a copse of banyan trees. As she plucked a few of the larger ones to add to her collection, she heard a loud screech from overhead. In the top branches of the next tree over, a brilliantly colored peacock ruffled its feathers as it preened its wings. Something on the branch glinted in the sunlight, creating a rainbow of dappled light on the ground.

Curious, Daijera pulled Epi's ribbon out of her hair, tied the flowers together, and carefully tucked the bouquet into her bag. She tied her split skirt to the side and scrambled up the trunk, stabilizing herself using the multitudes of anchored vines. The earthy scent of the tree filled her nostrils as she climbed, and she flashed back to her childhood.

"Don't get lost," Daijera's mother said from her sickbed as the *rambunctious five-year-old skipped out the door, grateful that someone had come to sit with Mother while she recovered from her illness. Sitting in a dark, stuffy room was boring.*

"I won't! I'll stay where I can see the house, I promise!" She had no intention of honoring the promise, of course, but it would make Mother feel better about letting her go and play.

Beside the isolated cabin, a massive banyan tree spread its wooden tentacles throughout the clearing, and Daijera imagined it as a kingdom of fairies, of which she could be queen. Its low-hanging branches made the climb easy, even for a child her size, and before long, she found herself nearly 20 feet off the ground. She gathered the fig-like fruit in her pockets and feasted while making up clever rhymes about the tiny brownies and pixies in her imaginary kingdom.

A squawk from the peacock brought her out of her reverie.

"Well, you don't have to stay," she told the bird as she straddled the limb. It cocked its head to one side, then the other, but made no effort to move. "Fine, then. Don't complain." She reached into a hollow space between two fused trunks, and her hand closed around the shiny object which had caught her attention.

The object felt somewhat rounded, and Daijera had to wiggle it carefully to release it from the tree's grasp. She tugged lightly, careful not to lose her balance.

"*Brrrah aya aya aya!*" She jumped as the peacock opened its mouth and cawed.

"That isn't very helpful, thank you," Daijera informed the bird, "and why do your lot always sound like cats? Shouldn't a beautiful bird have a beautiful voice?"

The peacock clucked in indignation.

"Don't take offense, bird. You're the one that tried to kill me by startling me off this branch."

Daijera looked down at the object clutched in her fingers, and was surprised to find herself holding a small vase. Though some of the brass was slightly tarnished, she could just make out the delicate etchings covering its surface. Tiny ivy was carved over the surface of the vase, intermingled with images of every manner of animal: goats, lions, horses, beetles…every creature she sought, she found.

Around the lip of the vase, a snake with intricate markings curved gracefully, and she found herself smiling to think that *her* animal was so prominently displayed. She studied the markings, trying to work out what species it was. The markings were unlike any she had seen: no repeating pattern, but clearly not random either.

The sky had begun to glow orange with the first hints of sunset, making the brass vase appear almost copper. Daijera looked toward the sun as it began to creep toward the horizon. It was the golden hour, when everything looks a little more beautiful, a little more healthy, a little warmer.

She turned back to the vase, and was alarmed to find it gone, and the peacock gone with it. Disoriented, she searched around the nearby branches and looked down toward the distant ground, fearing that she may have dropped it, but alas, it was as though it had never been there to begin with, a figment of her imagination like the fairies of her childhood.

Reaching for one of the sturdy tendrils so that she could make her way back to the ground, Daijera froze. Upon her wrist, the markings that had decorated the back of the snake were clearly visible, tinted black and green like a delicate tattoo.

She climbed down slowly and cautiously, lost in thought, then re-crossed the meadow to find Ren sitting up and drinking a cup of tea while Elia tried to tempt the bear cub away from him with an offering of honeycomb.

"Where did you make off to?" Xexia asked. It was more curiosity than criticism, but he had a suspicious look in his eye, as usual.

"I think I just had my Hohn test." She held out her wrist, and Xezia's eyebrows shot up as he examined the markings. "I'm glad to see you're feeling better, Ren."

"Right as rain," he chuckled as he watched the cub sniffing at Elia's attempt at bribery. "What have you got there?"

Daijera relayed an abbreviated version of the story. "I'm not sure what the snake's markings meant, but I feel like they're significant somehow."

"They're words." Xezia let go of Daijera's arm. "It's the same language we saw in Utrui's temple."

"Words? What does it say?" she asked.

"It says, *Have faith. Be bold.*"

"Well, that's very generic advice," Ekko commented. "I wonder what it means?"

"I suspect we shall find out before long." Dalgis stood and stretched his legs. "Shall we continue our journey? I have a sense that Hohn is waiting for us."

"What makes you think that, Dalgis?" Argus began packing up his kettle and throwing dirt on the small fire he'd made.

"I couldn't say for sure, but the sun is setting, and it feels like She is telling us our journey is nearing its conclusion."

Ren gingerly made his way to his feet and scooped the cub up in his arms. "Well, then, let's get a move on. We shouldn't keep the Goddess waiting."

Daijera fell silent as the words on her wrist rang through her with a meaning the others wouldn't understand. *Have faith, Daijera*, Hohn was saying. *Don't leave them. Not yet.* That wasn't what the words said, but Daijera was sure that's what they were saying to *her*.

Have faith.

A tall order for a woman who believed in nothing but survival and cleverness.

Have faith.

Argus

This place made no sense.

It was nearly impossible to plan, strategize, or even think properly in this mess of a realm. He meant no offense to Hohn in thinking this way, but not knowing what to expect, at least in general terms, made it very difficult to function. And what's more, it could have cost Ren his life.

The sooner they could acquire Hohn's book and get back to Talam, the happier Argus would be.

He looked back at Ren. The knight had turned his cloak into a makeshift sling, and the bear cub's curious eyes and snout poked out of the top of it, occasionally snuffling the air as they walked along.

"So, Ren, what is it that you plan to do with that cub?" Argus tried not to sound frustrated, but it seemed like no one else seemed to think through the consequences of their actions. "You can't exactly keep it as a pet."

Ren smiled broadly, as if he hadn't been mauled by a grizzly a mere hour earlier. "I'm sure Hohn will present a solution. But I couldn't very well just leave it all alone. It's too small."

Argus ground his teeth, knowing it was pointless to argue the flaws in Ren's logic. Talking to this group was like talking to children.

It was evident that each member of the group was being tested in some way, though the tests seemed random and without clear objectives, at least to his way of thinking. Elia's test seemed somewhat straightforward: she had to choose the correct path, but shouldn't that have been based on reasoning or some knowledge of cardinal directions? And then Dalgis's task seemed to have something to do with sacrifice, but what a ridiculous way to test whether or not someone would put themselves at risk for the greater good. Ren's task might have been related to bravery, but what a foolish, wasteful, and redundant set of circumstances, especially considering that no one questioned the man's mettle. And Daijera climbed a tree and got a tattoo? What was the point of that?

And perhaps the worst part of it all was that none of them questioned the chaos. Quite the contrary–they all seemed quite content, as though they had overcome some great obstacle.

Aggravating. All of it.

When they left the meadow, they had set out the way Daijera had gone earlier, through the grove of banyan trees. The grove seemed interminable, and made passage difficult because of the sprawling above-ground root systems. Each of the massive trees had large central trunks and then multiple other trunks extending down from the branches. Daijera had said this strange construction was the result of roots that dropped down from branches as they extended outward, then grew and hardened, thus allowing the banyans to spread outward almost indefinitely.

Under different circumstances, Argus would have found the trees fascinating, as he had never seen their like before. He might have to plan a family vacation to Heavenly Skies when he finally was able to return home. It would be fun for him and Sier to have a picnic near a tree like this, allowing the twins to climb and explore. Such a place would seem like a wonderland to them, so very different from the towering pines that made up the woodland areas near Breadstone.

He was distracted from his daydream by the sound of high laughter. He shot a look backwards, but both Elia and Ekko were lost in their own thoughts, and clearly weren't the source of the sound.

"Did you hear that?" he asked Xezia.

"Hear what?"

"Laughter. It sounded like it was coming from the trees over there."

"Probably some dryads or something," Xezia offered. "A place like this would be paradise for them."

It was a sensible suggestion, but somehow it didn't feel right. From up ahead, the sound came again, rippling through the forest like tinkling bells. It tugged at the edges of Argus's memory.

"I heard it that time." Xezia's eyes were fixed to the left toward the origin of the sound. Argus relaxed the tension in his jaw that he hadn't realized had been intensifying. "Should we check it out?"

"I feel like maybe we should, though I don't know why."

"Did anyone else hear someone laughing in the trees?" Elia called from the back of the group. Everyone nodded.

"I suspect it's significant that everyone noticed it. Let's go see what Hohn's cooking up for us now." Xezia started moving left, scanning the branches for hints of dryads or other forest-dwellers.

It wasn't long before they came to a tree far larger than the others. Its enormous central trunk was perhaps 20 feet across, and as they approached, they noticed something else: a door. While many banyans had large hollow areas, this one appeared to have been transformed into a dwelling of some sort.

The door was made of a darker and stouter wood than the banyans offered, two bands of studded iron holding the planks firmly together. In place of a knob, a large, turnable iron ring encircled a sizable keyhole.

"I guess we know they aren't faeries," Xezia remarked, gesturing at the iron fittings on the door.

More giggles, softer this time, and accompanied by a *shush, shush* trickled out from small windows several feet above the door.

"Hello, there," called Argus. The unintelligible sounds of children in whispered conspiracy were the only response. Argus knocked on the door, amused by the childish antics. "Is anyone at home?"

There was no response from within, and without prompting, Ekko leapt off of Dalgis's back onto a branch. She made her way to the trunk, attempting to peer into the windows. Then she pressed her ear against the glass.

"The curtains are drawn, and these windows don't appear to open from the outside," she reported. "I do hear movement in there, though." At the sound of her voice, a small human face appeared in the window, with large blue eyes and tousled blond hair.

Argus froze and closed his eyes, counted to three, then looked back, but the curtain had dropped back into place. "It can't be."

Xezia turned over his shoulder to look at Argus, somewhat disconcerted by the unnerved tone in the older man's voice. "Can't be what?"

"The face of the child in the window...he looked like my son Nevin. Not at his current age, but when he was about five."

"I guess we've stumbled across your test, Argus," Xezia quipped, clapping him on the back.

The tension in his jaw had returned. He didn't appreciate Hohn's sense of humor, if that's what this was. Her attempt to throw him off balance by presenting him with something that meant the world to him was a basic manipulation tactic, and he wasn't going to allow it to cloud his judgement. He knocked on the door again.

"Please come down, children!" There was no response. He thought back to games of hide and seek when the twins were small; they always hid together, even though that made hiding spots much more difficult for them to find. That said, they had been quite good at the game, and often stayed hidden even after Argus had called them in, telling them the game was over. He had admonished them for that, but Lifandi had argued that he could have been lying, trying to cheat them out of victory. Thereafter, he would have to announce that they won in order to get them to come out.

But this wasn't Breadstone, and these weren't his children.

"Whoa!" Ekko leapt down from her branch. "Something's happening!"

From the distant branches inward, a fungus of some sort was spreading with alarming speed. Black and yellow spores multiplied and spread, and infected leaves began to fall off the branches in bunches. The smell of wet rot began to fill the air.

"Children, you need to come out of there," Argus called, his voice rising. "Your tree is unsafe! We are friends, and will escort you out of danger. Please come out!"

Again, there was no response, and the mold continued to blacken the branches, which weakened and began to sag downward under their own weight.

"I think we should go in and get them." Elia stepped forward and tried twisting the ring. "Of course, it's locked."

"We shall have to break it down, then." Dalgis stepped forward. "Give me a little room here, friends." He turned his back to the door, preparing to mule-kick it off its hinges. "If you are near the door, children, you should stand clear! This door is going to come flying inward!" He shifted his weight forward, kicking hard against the door with his powerful back legs.

The door didn't budge, though the entire tree shook with the force of his kick.

There was a loud *SNAP* from behind them as a now-diseased branch broke free. It crashed to the ground only a few feet from where Daijera and Ren stood. The bear cub cowered in the sling. The rot had reached the trunk of the tree and began devouring the bark, spreading ever upward, and outward.

Screams erupted from within the tree house.

Despite his determination to be rational, panic rose within Argus. *They aren't Lifandi and Nevin,* he told himself, *but they are children. They must be taken out of danger at whatever cost!*

He began pounding on the door with all his strength. "Open this door at once!" he shouted, but his voice was drowned out by the sounds of terror inside.

The great tree began to groan with strain as its heavy branches began collapsing. All of Argus's reason and logic and training left him and he yanked on the door handle as if he could will it to open. He pounded on the door with both fists, oblivious to the pain of the jarring impact. He felt panicked tears pricking at the backs of his eyes as the sounds of Nevin and Lifandi's desperate voices filled his ears.

Suddenly Ekko was beside him and laid her hand on his trembling arm. She looked up at him, half his size, nearly still a child herself. He turned his eyes to her, wild with helplessness and grief.

"Try this," she said softly, drawing an enormous golden key out of her bag.

Some part of the back of his mind wondered where the key had come from and how she got it, but he grabbed the key from her outstretched hand and thrust it into the lock. He turned the key sharply, feeling the tumblers fall into place. Then he grabbed the iron ring and twisted it, and with a *click*, the door swung inward.

Argus rushed forward, intending to find and sweep up the children, then make a run for it. But the interior of the tree was no longer a tree. He looked around wildly, only slowly registering that the frightened children, the fungus, and the entire banyan forest were also gone. The only sounds were the quickened breath of the party and the *drip drip drip* of water somewhere nearby.

As his eyes adjusted to the sudden darkness, he found the source of the dripping...droplets of water were condensing on a mighty stalactite and dripping into a small pool of phosphorescent liquid, its gentle glow illuminating the walls of the cave.

A cave? The forest had disappeared and now they were in a cave.

"Dammit, Hohn!" thundered Argus, his expletive echoing against the walls of the cavern.

Chapter 14

The Wyrm

Xezia

He scanned the interior of the cavern with a mixture of annoyance and trepidation. Xezia knew that whatever came next was his trial to solve, and on the one hand, he just wanted to get it over with. On the other hand, though, he knew that he couldn't handle things as he always had.

Epi's warning echoed in his head: *I can help you, but you'll lose the use of any powers granted to you by Ipthel. If you use them, the corruption will return.*

How was he to know which of his powers came from Ipthel? He had to assume it was all of them; that was the only way to be sure the infection didn't take hold again. What did he have left to him if his magic was gone?

"Which way do you suppose we go now, Elia?" Dalgis wandered around the cavern and poked his head into the three dark tunnels leading away from this spot. "It's terribly dark in every direction."

"I'm not sure." Elia stepped in front of each opening, perhaps hoping to feel a tug on the instincts that had led her this far.

Xezia was somewhat surprised that she hadn't put the pattern together. "It doesn't matter which way we go, Elia. You've already had your trial, and for whatever reason, you were supposed to realize that you can make decisions and lead, and that people will follow you. Now that you've established that, Hohn will place the next obstacle in whichever direction you lead us."

177

Everyone turned to Xezia as if he'd just uttered a complete revelation, but he couldn't understand why. It had been so obvious.

"By the stars, Xezia, that's positively inspired!" Ren laughed, clapping him on the shoulder. The bear cub poked its head out of the sling and yawned.

Stig jumped out of Argus's hood and down the edge of the sling, looking at the cub critically. He chirped in a clipped staccato, and the cub responded with a clicky purr. Seemingly satisfied, Stig climbed into the sling and settled himself beside the warm and furry cub. Argus raised an eyebrow, but said nothing. It was hard to tell if he was irritated, amused, or fascinated. It was nearly always hard to tell with Argus.

"I don't know. It seemed pretty clear to me."

"What do you think was the purpose of the other trials?" Argus asked. "I've been struggling to see the logic in them."

Xezia shrugged. "Hohn certainly knows things we don't, so I wouldn't expect that it would all make sense to us. But it's evident that She is trying to make a point to each of us, more than to test us."

"Go on."

"So Dalgis's trial wasn't about strength, or even sacrifice, I don't think. Neither of those issues were in question. Dalgis, why did you lean into the wall and give up trying to get over it?"

Dalgis seemed surprised at the question. "I remembered how my father sacrificed himself for me, a memory that has haunted me everyday of my life. I felt as though I had abandoned him, failed him. But now I was in his shoes, so to speak. He knew that the only way to save me was for me to go on without him, as much as he wanted for things to be otherwise. But there was no other way. This was much the same. I wanted to go with you, but I resigned myself to the fact that the only thing I could do to help you succeed was to stay behind."

Xezia nodded. "So you carried the guilt of his death with you your whole life?"

"I did indeed."

"But you feel differently now?"

"Perhaps not entirely, but there is a new perspective for me to consider. I would not have wanted you to feel guilt for leaving me behind. It was simply the only way."

"So you surrendered to that knowledge, as your father did."

"Yes, I suppose you could phrase it that way."

"I believe, Dalgis, that your lesson is there. Hohn is trying to teach us, not test us."

"And what of Ren's test?" Argus prodded. "None of us would have questioned his mettle either, yet he could have been killed fighting that bear."

"I agree that is a mystery. Ren, what did you feel as your trial progressed?"

The knight considered the question. "I couldn't say precisely. I only knew that I had to protect Elia from the bear's attack at all costs. It was my sworn duty, and I felt as though I should die rather than fail in that duty."

"And why is that progression of thoughts significant?"

Ren paused. "I'm not sure I know."

"Yes, you do," Daijera interjected, her eyes meeting his in silent understanding.

"Ah, yes, perhaps so," he said softly. "I failed in my duty once before, a long time ago. This time, I did not fail."

"Surely that can't be all," Argus argued. "Ren has fought many battles, and has no doubt protected many people without regard to his own safety."

"Just so," Xezia replied. "Why was this time different?"

Ren pursed his lips, as though he could not allow the words in his heart to escape.

"Because the failure that haunts you was the failure to protect a young girl," Daijera offered, laying her hand on Ren's arm. He nodded, but could not speak. "This time, you did not fail," she smiled, and the tension in his face eased.

"Now, Ekko, suppose you tell us about that key..."

She met Xezia's eyes with hard resolve. "You don't need to know anything about it. All you need to know is that I was there to help Argus when he needed it."

The mage chuckled. "If you say so. Just so long as you learned whatever Hohn had intended for you. Daijera? *Be bold. Have faith.* What does that mean to you?"

Her eyes were clouded with her typical evasiveness. An edge crept into her voice. "I have never had faith in anything but myself. Perhaps Hohn wants me to expand my horizons."

"I'm certain there's more to it than that, aren't you?"

She shot Xezia a seething look, as though he had betrayed her by asking the question. "If there is, I shall sort through it on my own, thank you very much."

"Don't you think that, perhaps, that could be the point? To have faith in others? In your friends?"

Her look hardened, and all traces of emotion, even anger, disappeared behind a mask of impassivity. "I thank you for your concern, Xezia. Should I need counsel or advice, I know just who to turn to." Her tone was light, but final. He decided that pursuing his analysis would not only be fruitless, but she would likely view it as a violation of the Code. He wondered in passing what Epi would have to say about his continued involvement in the Black Moon, then shook that line of thought away to be addressed at a later time.

"What about you, Argus? That last episode was horrifying. Especially, I should think, for a father."

"I believe," the wizard replied in measured tones, "that Hohn was trying to remind me that there are certain scenarios that could cloud my reason, as much as I'd like to think I'm above frivolous emotionality." He flicked his fingers experimentally. "I think I should make you all aware of the fact that I don't seem to be able to spellcast here. No doubt more of Hohn's shenanigans."

A lump formed in Xezia's throat. *What am I without my magic?* "That seems both likely and highly inconvenient. Your analysis of your trial is very well reasoned, sir. I suspect there may be more to it than that, but I also believe you'll continue to ruminate on the subject until you squeeze every last drop of wisdom from it." Xezia smiled broadly, trying to dispel the air of discomfort that all the introspection had brought upon the group.

"I wonder what your trial will teach *you*." Ekko fished a torch out of the bag Dalgis carried around his neck. "Alright, Elia, if Xezia is right, then any direction will do. Which way do you want to go?"

The girl gazed into the pool, studying the veins of glowing crystal creating the weak light. "I think this way." Elia indicated the tunnel closest to the pool. "If Xezia is wrong, then I think I should select the way that seems different from the others. This path has sort of a landmark lighting the way, don't you think?"

"Good enough for me," Ekko agreed, using a tinderbox and small bottle of oil to light the torch. "Let's go see what Hohn has in store for Xezia."

Once they had left the cavern and its luminescent pool behind, the darkness pressed in upon them. Argus carried the torch and walked in front, and the rest of the line seemed to be graduated by how well each of them could see in the dark.

The tunnel, like the others, was wide and somewhat rounded and even, quite comfortable even for Dalgis's girth. The uniformity of the shape was highly unusual for caves, and struck Xezia as significant. "Argus, what do you make of this tunnel? Doesn't it seem unusually symmetrical?"

"I noted that as well. What are you thinking? Lava tubes?"

Xezia shook his head. "I doubt it. This is the wrong kind of rock. I don't see any evidence of heat or pressure here."

"What about those crystals? Wouldn't that imply igneous rock?"

"Ordinarily, yes, but we haven't seen any sign of other veins of that sort. This is more like marble. Look how smooth the sides are..."

"Water, then?"

"I doubt water would create this degree of similitude. The tunnel doesn't get larger or smaller. That doesn't seem natural to me."

"Agreed, but this is Hohn's domain. Everything here is natural."

"That's precisely what worries me." Xezia ran his tongue against the inside of his cheek as he thought. His concentration was broken by the sound of whispering behind him and then a shout from Dalgis.

"Have you gentlemen noticed the slight change in temperature?"

"No, Dalgis," Xezia called back. "What have you noticed?"

"Things seem marginally warmer. I deduce that there may be some sort of heat source up ahead. Ekko is volunteering to scout ahead since she sees exceptionally well in the dark."

Xezia wasn't sure if a heat source was a good thing or a bad thing, but having a little reconnaissance could only be helpful. "Thank you, Ekko." After she darted past him, his mind clamped down on what Dalgis had just said. *Why would Ekko's eyesight in darkness be any better than Argus's, Ren's, or Elia's?* He filed the thought away, vowing to solve the riddle at a later time.

After a few moments, Ekko returned. "Dalgis is right. There's a large cavern up ahead, and I think it might be our destination. It's...different from the tunnels. And there's something living in the tunnels, too. I don't think it was in the chamber, but I'm pretty sure it's nearby."

"What brought you to that conclusion?" Argus asked.

"I...well...you'll kind of have to trust me. But I have a pretty good nose, and it sort of smells like something has been through there."

"Please tell me it's not a dung heap," came Elia's voice from just outside the circle of torchlight.

"No, nothing like that. Just sort of a mossy, swampy smell which isn't really noticeable here. There's also another glowing pool up there, though it's really more like a puddle. It did create just enough light for me to see that the walls aren't smooth all the way around like these, and there is a big rock in the middle of the cavern."

"How big is the cavern?" Ren asked.

"I'd say maybe a quarter the size of the last one. Like the size of a typical shop. Maybe thirty feet across? But it wasn't even like the tunnels, so parts of it are smaller."

"Thank you for that report, Ekko. I think it would be wise to prepare for whatever may come. You may wish to draw your arms if you haven't already done so." Argus tried again to create sigils in the air, but no evidence of magic was forthcoming.

When they reached the cavern Ekko had described, Xezia took the torch from Argus and shone it around. If this was to be his trial, he might as well start getting a lay of the land. "You're right, Ekko, this isn't like the tunnel. In fact, there are two distinct types of rock here. The marble-like stone we've been seeing, and then this white stone here that starts in the center and then runs around the edge there."

He stepped forward to lay his hand on the white stone, which glowed golden in the glow of the torch.

"Xezia, wait–" Dalgis cried in alarm, but he was too late to stop Xezia's outstretched palm as it made contact with the unusual formation.

Which moved when he touched it.

"HOW *DARE* YOU?" came a booming voice, echoing off all the walls of the chamber.

Xezia jerked his hand back as the rock began to move.

Move?

He gazed wildly around the cavern, and it seemed like nearly half the walls were moving, undulating with slow, rippling vibrations. Across the chamber, a gargantuan head pulled backward out of an adjoining tunnel. The beast was eyeless, but more than made up for the deficit with a gaping maw of two inset rows of cone-shaped teeth, each as long as Xezia's forearm. Its tongue was ridged along the sides, and dripped with the luminescent liquid that gave the faintest light in the darkness. The huge muscular flap swung back and forth like the clapper of a sideways bell.

"WHO ARE YOU AND WHAT INSOLENCE BRINGS YOU TO MY LAIR?" The lips and tongue moved out of sequence with the words, and the message seemed to ripple through their minds more than through the air around them.

Xezia's blood ran cold, and the desire to flee gripped him, but a voice within him reminded him that this was his trial, his task to overcome. But how could a creature such as this be defeated, particularly without his magic?

"I am Xezia, mage of Epi. My friends and I have been led here by the hand of Epi Herself. We seek Hohn's Book." His voice was tremulous, but he managed to get the words out.

The chamber shook as the wyrm's coils vibrated with vicious laughter. "EPI HAS NO POWER HERE, MORTAL. AND EVEN IF SHE DID, SHE HAS NO DOMINION OVER THE BOOK OF LIFE."

"I meant no disrespect..."

"YOUR VERY PRESENCE HERE IS DISRESPECT."

"Surely Hohn is aware of our presence. She has tested each of us on our approach to this place." He struggled to find the right words to say.

A rivulet of the glowing saliva dripped off of the beast's tongue and plopped onto the stone floor. As Xezia watched, the marble around the liquid corroded slightly, creating a pool about the size of his fist.

"DO I LOOK LIKE HOHN TO YOU?"

The insulting tone grated against Xezia's mind, cutting through the terror and awareness of the danger he was in. His whole life, such had been the case. Attitude nearly always won over good sense.

"I couldn't say. I don't know what Hohn looks like."

The walls rippled with laughter again. "YOU ARE BOLD, I WILL GIVE YOU THAT. FACED WITH DEATH, YOU CHOOSE IMPUDENCE AS YOUR WEAPON. I AM ALMOST AMUSED."

Xezia felt a thump on his back and turned to see that Daijera had slipped up beside him.

Negotiate, she mouthed silently.

UNDERSTANDING WASHED over him. Over and over he had asked what was left of him without his magic, and here was the answer, the very trait that had caused Ipthel to target him to begin with: his cleverness.

"I fear that we may have gotten off on the wrong foot..." Xezia began.

"I DO NOT HAVE FEET, YOU DOLT." And then the coils rumbled. The creature was laughing at its own joke.

"Of course not. Please forgive my crude colloquialisms. Allow me to begin again..."

"WHY WOULD I DO THAT? YOU ARE INSIGNIFICANT BUGS NEXT TO ONE SUCH AS MYSELF. I COULD DISSOLVE YOU WHERE YOU STAND."

Xezia didn't doubt that this was true, but he swallowed hard and continued. "I can see that you are a being of great power, and my friends and I are certainly in awe of your magnificence." When the wyrm did not respond, Xezia pushed on. "We are on a mission of great importance to the outside world, and our quest has led us here."

"WHAT CARE I FOR THE OUTSIDE WORLD?"

"Surely not at all, and there is no reason why you should. But Hohn must care somewhat, if She allowed us this far. I assume you are well acquainted with Her?"

"NATURALLY." After a short pause, the walls shook as the wyrm laughed at its own pun. It seemed to like amusing itself with its own wit.

"You are very clever," Xezia purred. "No doubt that is why She led us to you. Do you know where we can find the Book of Life?"

"OF COURSE I DO, PUNY MAN. HOHN HAS ENTRUSTED IT INTO MY KEEPING FOR AN EON."

"A wise choice on Her part, as no one could take it from you against your wishes, for no one is mighty enough." The wyrm was silent again, and it was clear that it enjoyed the flattery. "Could we persuade you to part with it? Particularly since it seems to be Her will?"

"YOU HAVE NO PLACE ASSUMING THAT YOU UNDERSTAND HOHN'S WILL, INSECT."

"Indeed, I would not presume to do so. I am simply using deductive reasoning to conclude that She brought us to you with this in mind. Where are my manners? I have told you my name, but I have not asked you for yours. Terribly rude of me."

"INDEED IT WAS. I AM ALABASTER."

"Oh! Named for the stone?"

"HOHN NAMED THE STONE AFTER *ME*, IDIOT."

"Of course She did. How silly of me. And She made it just your color as well. She must think a great deal of you."

Alabaster did not speak, but there was a *thump thump* from the distant end of his enormous body.

"Can we, perhaps, negotiate a trade with you? Is there some service we can provide you in exchange for the book?"

'WHAT A RIDICULOUS NOTION. YOU HAVE NOTHING I DESIRE. RICHES MEAN NOTHING TO ME. THERE IS NO TASK YOU COULD DO THAT I COULD NOT EASILY ACCOMPLISH MYSELF IF I WISHED."

Xezia's brain whirled. It was true that they had nothing Alabaster would value, except...

"It does seem an awful shame that one so great as you is kept hidden from the world." Would the wyrm rise to the bait?

"I AM NOT HIDDEN. THIS IS MY HOME."

"Ah, but the world is poorer for not knowing your greatness."

"I HAD NOT THOUGHT OF THAT, BUT IT IS TRUE. STILL, IT IS OF NO MATTER TO ME."

"Wouldn't it be grand, though, if my friend Daijera here were to compose an ode extolling your glory? She is a gifted performer, and she could spread 'The Ballad of Alabaster' across the world in her travels. Then everyone in the four kingdoms would know your name and fear you!"

Alabaster cocked its head to one side and clicked its teeth together as it considered this. "OR I COULD JUST CRUSH YOU ALL TO MUD AND FEAST ON YOUR REMAINS."

"You could indeed, and I doubt there is much we could do to stop you. But I believe there is much more to be gained with my suggestion."

"YOU ARE A FUNNY CREATURE. STUPID AND ARROGANT, BUT FUNNY. PERHAPS I SHALL EAT YOU, PERHAPS NOT. THE BOOK IS HERE." Alabaster's great head slid to the left, revealing a niche carved into the wall. Within the niche, tucked safely next to the jaw of Alabaster, sat a tome wrapped in flowering vines. "WHY DON'T YOU TAKE IT FROM ME, THEN, IF YOU ARE SO CERTAIN IT IS HOHN'S WILL?" The beast's thin lips curled back from the nightmare of pointed teeth. It's tongue flicked back and forth in anticipation.

Xezia looked back at the group. Each of them gripped weapons: Argus and Ren carried swords, Ekko and Elia gripped daggers, Dalgis's claws were at the ready, and Daijera's cheeks were swollen, her venom sacs full. But looking at Alabaster, it was clear that an army of fighters could not prevail over this creature. No, that was not the solution.

"WHY DO YOU HESITATE, INSECT? DO YOU NOT BELIEVE WHAT YOU SAID? THAT HOHN HERSELF WISHES YOU TO SUCCEED?"

The mage shot a sideways glance at Daijera as he tried to work out what he was meant to do. Suddenly he stood stock straight as the realization crashed down on him. He grabbed the lamia's wrist and stared at the tattoo.

Be bold. Have faith. Perhaps that message had not been for her alone.

He turned back to Alabaster.

"WELL, INSECT?" The wyrm licked its lips, leaving a phosphorescent trail that oozed over its teeth.

Xezia took a deep breath, said a silent prayer to Epi, and stepped toward Alabaster's giant head. Each step forward brought him closer to the Book, and to razor-sharp death.

"YES, DO COME CLOSER." Alabaster clacked its teeth together and Xezia could smell its breath: a scent of earth and decay.

Only three more steps, two, and then he could reach the Book.

Alabaster snapped its head sharply in Xezia's direction, so the mage did the only thing he could think to do: he grabbed the Book from the alcove and ran down the nearest tunnel, trusting that his companions would follow.

The walls of the labyrinth of caverns shook with the sound of Alabaster's roar, and there was a great scratching and sliding sound which must have been the great body moving along the walls. Xezia could barely hear the many running feet behind him over the sound of his own pounding heart.

He was running in the darkness, with no sense of his surroundings. Several times he stumbled, but he did not stop.

What was that? *Light!* A weak but warm glow up ahead heralded the end of the tunnel. Adrenaline shot through his body, and he was vaguely aware that he shouted something about the light to the people running behind him.

Suddenly he burst into the open, the light emanating from the crystals blinding him after the prolonged darkness. He chanced to cast a glance over his shoulder, hoping that everyone had escaped Alabaster's fury. Dalgis burst into view, having been trying to protect the party by bringing up the rear, and behind him, the stone wall rippled. A final roar echoed from the mountain, and then the entrance to the tunnel was simply gone.

The wall of the cavern was solid and unblemished, as if the tunnel had never existed, and Xezia's knees crumpled underneath him. He knelt on the stone ground of the city of Talam, next to Solaris's shop.

Xezia did not attempt to rise until his breath and his heart calmed. It was only then that he remembered that he clutched the Book of Hohn to his chest.

Chapter 15

Celebration

Elia

"Tonight's party will be wonderful!" Epi gushed. "I'm so glad I wore my pretty dress!" She was sitting on Solaris's shoulders, braiding his black hair and tying it up with ribbons. Though his teeth were gritted, he endured the Goddess' attentions patiently.

"How is it possible that we haven't missed the feast?" Ren was dangling one of Epi's ribbons in front of the bear cub, which was on its back pawing at the bright-colored fabric. "We were walking in Hohn's demesnes for hours!"

"Oh, time passes as We wish it to in Our own domains. I'm sure She didn't want you to miss the celebration. It *is* in your honor, after all."

"That was, of course, assuming you survived. I didn't give you very strong odds, to be honest." Solaris's tone was one of grudging respect. "Alabaster must have been off its game today. Either that, or it let you escape."

"I have no doubt that Alabaster could have crushed us or dissolved us at any time, had that been his intention." Solaris had opened up the back wall, and Dalgis sat next to Xezia, who was still cradling the Book of Life in his arms. The flowering vines that encircled it kept growing up and over Dalgis's shoulders and tickling his chin until he munched the twisting leaves back down to their source. Once he swallowed, the vines would grow back. He took another bite. "That will be quite enough, thank you, Book. I am quite satiated." The vines wrapped themselves tightly around the Book and exploded into bloom, making

193

it appear that Xezia held a large bouquet of wildflowers. "Simply marvelous."

"I think that maybe you should keep the book in your satchel, Dalgis," the mage said, just a touch of wistfulness in his voice. "It seems to...like you."

"I should be most honored, Xezia. I shall protect it with my life."

"That is a stupendous idea, Xezia!" Epi chirped. "And may I say that you did very well on your trial. Hohn let me watch you as long as I promised not to help."

"Thank you," he replied meekly, but with genuine pleasure in his tone. "I have to admit that I'm grateful not to be wyrm food."

Epi's tinkly laughter filled the back room of the shop. "Oh, that old Alabaster is a big old bully. It wouldn't have eaten you. It only eats rocks and dirt."

"So we were never actually in danger?" Ekko lay sprawled on Solaris's bed with her head hanging upside down over the edge.

"I didn't say that. It could have killed you, but it wouldn't have eaten you. I'm pretty sure Hohn had told it not to kill you, though."

"Pretty sure?"

"Yeah, pretty sure."

Daijera began picking out notes on her lute. Then she cleared her throat and burst into a singsong limerick:

> There once was a wyrmie of old
> That thought it was clever and bold
> It guarded a Book
> Which we just now took
> A treasure more precious than gold

Peals of laughter erupted from the entire group, more of relief and exhaustion than actual mirth.

"I'm definitely going to repeat that to the old earthwyrm next time I visit." Solaris cracked the slightest smile.

Epi burst into a fit of giggles. When she caught her breath, she climbed down from her perch and twirled her skirts in a billowy circle before making her way over to Elia. "I think you should open the letter now!" She climbed into Elia's lap. "Read it out loud."

Elia drew the folded parchment from her bag and broke the sparkly pink wax seal. The words were written in the same color ink, and Elia had to angle the paper for better light. The handwriting was elegant and precise, definitely not the script of a child. She reminded herself that Epi chose to appear as a tiny girl, but She could just as easily present Herself as a dragon, an ancient sorcerer, or a ray of light. Elia began to read aloud.

To my dear new friends,

You have, each for your own reasons, embarked on a life path which will alter each of you. You will learn what lies in your heart, what you value, and what you are capable of. Each of you is at a critical crossroads in your life, and who you were before this moment no longer defines you. You are who you choose to be. And it gives me great joy to walk some part of this path with you.

Know that all the Deities are aware of you, but not all of Them are on your side. Some will remain removed and distant, but that does not mean They don't support you. Immortals have a different perspective, and Our actions might not always make sense to you. But know that, with the possible exception of Rahmgn, every action has a purpose, for good or for ill. Trust your highest self and it will tell you what to do.

I will support you when I can, but even I have limitations to how much I may interfere in the affairs of mortals.

My advice to you is this: proceed next to try to meet with my sister Hoshkn. She is very wise—perhaps the wisest of us all. While there are many ways into Her kingdom, there is a village in central Benedictus called Halasa. There is a very special statue dedicated to Hoshkn there, and a large burial yard beyond. I believe if you go there, you will find your way to my Sister's house.

I have one request of you. On the northmost coast of Benedictus, there is a tiny fae fishing village called Epon. The residents there have been most devoted to Me for centuries, and I love them dearly. Please visit them and bring them my greetings. They have suffered much, not so much because of the war, but because of the piracy that has run rampant since Godfroy's fool crusade began. Do something to bring them joy, so they may know that I watch over them, though I cannot prevent all the misfortune that comes their way.

I believe in you, friends. Go forth and do great things.

With my whole heart,

Epi

There was a tear in Elia's eye when she finished reading. She struggled to respond because so many questions were spinning around in her brain, and she feared offending the Goddess with nonsense.

Epi giggled and threw her arms around Elia's neck. "You do know I can hear you, right? You are a nice person, Elia. Would you like to be my friend?"

The question was one a child would ask, but the eyes that probed Elia's were ancient and full of the deepest knowledge. "Yes, Epi, I would very much like to be your friend."

"Yay! We will be best friends forever!" Epi crushed her in a hug that nearly cut off her ability to breathe, but she didn't mind. Her heart fluttered with happiness and peace.

Epi broke the hug and slid off Elia's lap. She skipped over to Xezia, who was watching with sad and wistful eyes.

"Don't worry, Xezia, I still love you, too! I can have many friends. I'm a goddess, after all! And you belong to Me now!" She planted a solid kiss on his cheek.

"Oh, don't misunderstand, my lady. I am not jealous. I..." He was unable to finish his sentence, and his eyes fell.

"You are missing Sora." It was not a question, and he did not deny it. "I do not know where she is, Xezia, I'm sorry. She is hidden from me.

But I was thinking of you when I chose your destination. I have sent you to the temple in Halasa. Do you know why?" He shook his head and raised his questioning eyes to Hers. "The temple at Halasa is very special to Sora. Find Hoshkn with the purple shoes, and you shall be where your dear Sora once was, many years ago."

80
Argus

He meant no disrespect to the storm elves, but Argus was not in the mood for revelry. Hohn's test for him had taught him that there was one thing that could erode his careful sense of logic: his family.

And he missed them more than ever.

He wanted to get this damned quest over with and return to his wife, his twins, and his tavern. And, of course, his studies.

There was much to be done, and he did not want to waste time with frivolity. So he sat at the kitchen table in the house they had been given for the night with his map spread in front of him. He began making a list in his journal.

1. Return to Verwoerd
2. Collect Lock and Damien
3. Visit Epon (fae village)
4. Military research facility?
5. Go to cemetery in Halasa
6. Connect with Hoshkn?
7. Check in on Aerith?
8. Get Stig some bloodworms

Argus set down the pen and rubbed his eyes. This quest seemed interminable. At a bare minimum, this list represented almost two weeks of travel, and that only accounted for half of the Holy Books. And what then? How were the books safer with them than hidden and scattered around the world?

"Ah, here you are," came a voice from the doorway.

"Hello, Ren. Are you enjoying the party?"

"Well, I admit that I greatly enjoyed the venison. Something about the salt the storm elves use...very unique. Why are you sequestered away in this cottage, friend?"

"I'm just trying to figure out the most logical sequence of events."
Argus beckoned Ren over to the map, somewhat grateful to have a
compatriot to talk to as he organized his thoughts. "We are here, more
or less, not too terribly far from the northern coast of Rosend.
Verwoerd is on our way to wherever else we might go next, but I am
torn between checking out that research facility Damien talked about
or heading for the fae village next. This Ebon Ichor is a menace, but
perhaps pursuing the Book of Death is the more immediate need.
What say you?"

Ren studied the map and considered, stroking his short beard
thoughtfully. "I suppose they are both important, but I am inclined to
think we should prioritize Epi's request and visit the fae village, then
seek the Book of Death. She is a goddess after all."

Argus nodded. "Sound reasoning. If she felt the Ichor was the
primary threat, she'd have mentioned it."

"That was my reasoning as well."

Stig hopped up on the table and looked at Ren expectantly. "Your
friend is outside with Ekko," he explained to the lizard. Stig chirruped
in response, then climbed up on the wizard's hand.

"Oh, all right," Argus sighed. "I don't suppose staring at this map is
going to make the time go any faster." He folded up the map and tucked
it in his journal, then slid both into his satchel. He looked up at Ren.
"Do you suppose there's any venison left?"

Ren chuckled. "Almost certainly. Come on, friend. Let us take one
evening to rest and renew our spirits, and we shall be in a better frame
of mind to begin our journey southward tomorrow."

The celebration was a simple, yet joyful affair. A long table had
been loaded up with foods of all kinds: fruits, berries, root vegetables,
and a variety of roasted meats. A storyteller had gathered children
around her, and seemed to be imparting tales of great adventure, if
the reactions of the audience were any indication. Dalgis sat amongst
them, and though Argus was fairly sure he was unable to understand

the storyteller's words, children perched on his back and curled around his legs, making him look like a large, tufted piece of furniture.

Daijera and her lute were positioned by the tree in the town square, and though he could not make out the words of her song, the lilt of her voice was just audible above the din. Ekko and Elia sat with the storm elf girl, who was holding up object after object, presumably trying to teach them the language so few other races had ever heard. Xezia was nowhere to be seen.

Ren clapped Argus on the shoulder and the two wandered over to the banquet table in silence.

Well, he supposed, being well-fed and well-rested could not be a bad thing. There would be many coming days when they would be neither, so perhaps it was wise to try and enjoy a brief respite after all.

Tomorrow, the search for the next Book would begin.

Their breakfast the next morning, as might be expected, consisted of leftovers from the banquet the night before. It wasn't a traditional breakfast by any means, but it was ideal for travelers about to head out on a long trek. Croia had succeeded in teaching Ekko and Elia a little bit of the storm elf language, and she named each of the travel-friendly foods as she put them in a satchel. The girls told her the Dyosa words in return.

Solaris knocked twice, then let himself into their borrowed common room. "Long journey ahead. Gidón and Croia will accompany you part of the way back to ensure you don't get lost."

"That's most generous of them," Argus replied. "I'm quite eager to get going."

Ren came down the stairs with the bear cub in his arms. "Ah, Solaris, good morning! We missed you at last night's festivities."

He smirked. "I'll wager you didn't. At any rate, I came to see you off and to speak to you about the cub."

Ren looked down at the wriggling creature in his arms. "I've been wondering about that. I can't very well take him with me, and he's too small to be left without care."

"It's even more complicated than that, actually. That cub is not of this world; it belongs in Hohn's domain. I've come to take it home."

"I can't say I won't miss the little cuss," Ren wrangled it onto its back and scratched its belly while the bear pawed and made nasal growling noises. "I am relieved, though, that it has a proper place to be. I couldn't see myself trying to convince Colvyn that it would be a fine idea to keep a bear in either a room or a stable."

"I imagine that would have been an interesting conversation to witness." The Guardian extended his arms, and Ren handed the cub over. Solaris looked at it with something almost like affection as it began nibbling on his fingertips. "I wish you a fair journey. You all have shown yourselves to be at least passably competent, and I hope you are successful. A word of advice, though. Keep an eye on that acolyte of Epi's. She has a bit of a soft heart and wants to see the best in everyone, but he's got a shiftiness to him I don't quite trust."

"Your advice is most welcome," Argus replied. "We shall take pains to keep him honest."

"You can do what you will, but the choice is his alone, and your road is a long one. Good fortune to you." Having said his peace, Solaris hoisted the cub onto his shoulder as a parent might carry an infant. Then he turned on his heel and strode out the door.

Preview

Ironshield's Shadow Part 4:
The Book of Death

Chapter 1
Killing the Past
Ekko

THE RAIN STARTED WHEN they were about two hours out from Verwoerd. Had Ekko been in fox form, she wouldn't have minded particularly. But being in human form with wet clothes was incredibly uncomfortable, and being uncomfortable made her very grumpy.

When they finally arrived at the Silver Branch Inn, it was all she could do to wait for their room keys. She fled upstairs and stripped off her wet clothes and shifted, then curled up on the bed, grateful to be dry and warm. She fell asleep almost instantly.

It was hard to tell how long she had been asleep, since the sky was gray and overcast. Her clothes hadn't dried appreciably, so she was guessing it hadn't been long. She yawned and stretched, then shifted back to her human body. She fished in her backpack for a spare set of clothes, then constructed a makeshift clothesline out of rope and hung her travel clothes out to dry.

As she reached out the window to dump the rainwater out of her boots, there was a quiet rapping at her door.

She opened it to find Damien standing on the threshold, a sheepish grin on his face.

"What are you doing here?" she demanded.

"I wanted to talk to you. Since we're going to be traveling together, I wanted to try and make peace."

"There's no peace to make, Damien. You can try and rationalize it away, but you left me to die in order to save your own skin. I want nothing to do with you. We're not friends, or anything else. That's not going to change because you have useful information."

"What if I told you I'd changed? That seeing my father die and my mother carted away had made me realize that I needed to change my life?"

"Then I'd say you're not only a liar, but a bastard to use your father's death as a sympathy chip. I'm sorry about your family, but that doesn't change what you are. You may even have redeeming moments now and then, but when it comes down to it, you're a rat, pure and simple."

"That's harsh, Ekko." He looked hurt, but she knew better.

"You know what's harsh? Having to shift in a jail cell, praying that no one would see me, and then run for my life. Right past the gallows where they meant to hang me for what YOU did, by the way. Don't talk to me about harsh."

"Look, I'm trying to make amends by helping you..."

"No, you're not. Even they don't believe that, and they don't know you like I do. You want out of your current situation, and you're willing to barter information to achieve that. And you know what? Fine. We'll take the deal, and then we'll pass you off somewhere else and you're on your own. I will endure your presence for as long as that part takes, but make no mistake about this, Damien: if you cross anyone in this party, there will be a line of people waiting to kill you, and you'd better hope I'm at the front. I'm a thief, so I'm not complicated. But some of these folks? They have a much more violent past than mine. You'd be wise to hold up your end of the deal and then disappear."

"Since when are you a team player?" He crossed his arms and leaned rakishly against the doorframe.

"Since it serves me for the moment, and since I'm part of something bigger than survival right now."

"What's bigger than survival?"

"Nice try. But you'll get no information out of me. Goodbye, Damien. We'll be riding in the same party, but we are NOT together. You'd be smart to remember that."

"What? Or you'll have that beast Dalgis eat me?"

"You'd be lucky to have that quick a death at his hands if you betray me." She shoved him back into the hallway and slammed the door. Just to ensure that he didn't just pick the lock and let himself in, she wedged a chair under the door latch to keep it secure.

Unfortunately, keeping him out had locked her in as well.

This had been a truly frustrating day so far. There had better be rabbit stew for dinner.

There was no rabbit, but there was roasted quail, and that was almost as good. Thankfully, Damien had been smart enough NOT to join them for dinner. The rain had slowed to a drizzle, so Ekko took her food out to the stables so she could eat with Dalgis.

"He seems to have truly gotten under your skin, if you don't mind my saying so," Dalgis observed, munching on flowers that had snaked their way out of his satchel and halfway across the stable.

"He killed a guy during a burglary, and then let me take the blame. Safe to say that I'm not about to let that go."

"Indeed, and I think that is wise. But surely, you've come across other less-than-trustworthy people in your life. Do they all upset you in this way?"

Ekko knew what he was getting at. "Of course not." She paused, not sure if she should tell the story, but one look at Dalgis's earnest face convinced her. "My childhood was...less than ideal."

"I imagined as much."

"Yeah, well, my parents sent me into town once a week, on market day, to pick pockets. I was really good at it, and I was a cute kid, so it was actually a pretty easy job. But they never let me keep any of it for myself. They took everything and sold what they could. They did buy food, but they also bought themselves nice things. My brother and I had the basics, but nothing fancy or nice. It wasn't fair."

"I can see how that would have upset you."

"So one time, I kept this necklace because I really liked it. I mean, I knew I couldn't wear it anywhere, because it might be recognized by somebody, but I just wanted to keep it. To have something pretty of my own."

"I am guessing you got caught hiding it?"

"My mother caught me. And when she did, she gave me a beating I wouldn't soon forget. I knew I wouldn't be of value much longer; I was getting old enough to be recognizable in the market, and that was really the only benefit my parents felt they got from me. I decided to get out before they kicked me out. I wanted to take my brother with me, but he wouldn't go. So I left without him."

"Were you close to your brother?"

"Yeah, well, I thought so. But then he decided he'd rather stay with *them* than come with me. Things were harder on my own than I thought they'd be, even if I spent a lot of my time as a fox. I was even considering going back, but then Damien found me. He'd been out on his own for a couple of years, and he taught me how to find places to stay, how to sell the stuff I stole, that kind of thing. We were a team, at least for a year or so."

"You loved him."

"I thought I did. He was an amazing con artist, but I thought he'd always play it straight with *me*. I was wrong. I was useful to him, and nothing more."

"That must have been very painful." Dalgis's eyes were soft with sympathy.

"It was. The truth is that if he'd asked me to take the fall because I could likely escape jail, or if he'd promised to help break me out, I'd probably have gone along with it. But he didn't. He abandoned me like I meant nothing to him. I had been convenient, and that meant I was replaceable. That's what I'll never forgive. He made me feel even worse than my parents did." She hugged her knees to her chest.

"You know that that part of your life is over now, right, Ekko? You have loyal friends now, and you keep company with deities. You have risen above what he and your parents made of you. You are your own person now, and you answer to no one."

Ekko looked up at Dalgis with wet eyes, then hugged his neck fiercely. "Will you still promise to gut him if he betrays us?"

"Without hesitation, little fox. Without hesitation."

The Deities of the Realm

Epi (Ep'-ee): Deity of Purity

Hohn (Hōn): Deity of Life

Hoshkn (Hōsh'-kĭn): Deity of Death

Ipthel (Ĭp'-thəl): Deity of Corruption

Utrui (Oo-troo'-ee): Deity of Order

Rahmgn (Rahm'-ghĭn): Deity of Chaos

The Adventurers

Argus (Ar'-gəs): Human. A wizard and one of the renowned Scholars of the Six, who resides and runs a tavern in Breadstone, in the north of Ironshield.

Daijera (Dī-jeer'-ə): Lamia. Resides in Nightveil, on the coast of Heavenly Skies. An agent of the Black Moon skilled at information brokering and the occasional assassination. By trade, a storyteller and musician.

Dalgis (Dahl'-ghĭs): Unique and un-named species, but dubbed a "pheonix lizard" by a child from Wheatfields. Nomadic, but originated in southwestern Ironshield. Was magically created by his "father", Yousef Gonestible, who was executed by King Godfroy for his magical/biological experiments.

Ekko (Ĕk'-ō): Werefox. Nomadic, but originally from central Rosend. A skilled young thief who has been living off of her wits since she was 12.

Elia (Ĕl'-lee-ə): Human. Orphaned as a child and raised by her Aunt Mita in Breadstone, in northern Ironshield. Trained as an herbalist before being conscripted into King Godfroy's army.

Ren (Rehn'): Human. Originally from northern Rosend, but raised in Davit, outside of Ironshield City. Trained to be a knight to the royal Talon family before the usurpation by King Godfroy.

Xezia (Zā'-zee-ə): Mixed race of sun elf, human, and orc. Mage of Epi. Ambitious agent of Black Moon, interested in rising to a position of power, ostensibly to bend the organization to less corrupt ways. Originally from a (now destroyed) village in eastern Heavenly Skies.

Sora (Sōr'-ə): Sun elf. Smuggler working for Black Moon who owes Xezia a blood debt, and thus must stay by his side until released from her vow. Raised in the town of Halasa in Benedictus.

Met Along the Way

Aarna (Ar'-nə): Black Moon agent disguised as a fortune teller

Alabaster (Al-ə-bass'-ter): A monstrous earthwyrm which lives in Hohn's domain

Colvyn (Kohl'-vinn): Elven innkeeper of the Silver Branch Inn in the town of Verwoerd. He is a childhood friend of Argus's.

Croia (Croy'-ə): A friendly storm elf warrior maiden

Damien (Day'-mee-en): Ekko's ex-boyfriend

Gidón (Gih-dohn'): Leader of the storm elf scouting party

Moraia (Mohr-eye'-ah): Guardian of Hohn and purveyor of a flower stand

Olifa (Oh-lee'-fə): Elder storm elf of Talam

Phelia (Fee'-lee- ə): Zealot leader of the Obsidian Skulls, a sorceress of arcane magic and devotee of Ipthel

Solaris (Soh-lahr'-iss): Guardian and Champion of Hohn, and a very grumpy shopkeeper

Yana (**Ora-ini**) (Yah'-nah, Or'-ah-ee'-nee): Grandmother of Colvyn and matriarch of the family

About the Co-Creators

Always pondering their next creative venture, **Lea Scism** is the type of person whose head would explode without a project to work on. Their journals are filled with stories and drawings about all manner of fantastical beings, from the wonderful to the horrifying. Previously shared only among friends, with the aid of like-minded writers like JB Caine and Sam Hamilton, they're now working on putting all that imagination before a wider audience.

Sam Hamilton has never been a writer. But D&D gave them a chance to create stories in a way that felt more obtainable. They found a love for playing D&D in high school with their friends and my first campaign and discovered a love of lore and side quests. Years later, they finally felt comfortable co-running a game with the amazing world-builder Lea Scism for the Speech & Debate team, and together they created a story that helped them fall in love with the game even more. With the talents of JB Caine, that game has come to life...a reality they never expected. They are so excited for the future as a player and as a DM.

Don't miss out!

Visit the website below and you can sign up to receive emails whenever JB Caine publishes a new book. There's no charge and no obligation.

https://books2read.com/r/B-A-OLWBB-EDYWC

Connecting independent readers to independent writers.

Milton Keynes UK
Ingram Content Group UK Ltd.
UKHW031040120324
439302UK00001B/101

9 798224 755578